Ruth

Classic British crime fiction is the best in the world—and Ruth Rendell is crime fiction at its very best. Ingenious and meticulous plots, subtle and penetrating characterizations, beguiling storylines and wry observations have all combined to put her at the very top of her craft.

Her first novel, *From Doon with Death*, appeared in 1964, and since then her reputation and readership have grown steadily with each new book. She has now received eight major awards for her work: three Edgars from the Mystery Writers of America; the Crime Writers' Gold Dagger Award for 1976's best crime novel for *A Demon in My View*; the Arts Council National Book Award for Genre Fiction in 1981 for *Lake of Darkness*; the Crime Writers' Silver Dagger Award for 1985's best crime novel for *The Tree of Hands*; the Crime Writers' Gold Dagger Award for 1986's best crime novel for *Live Flesh*, and in 1987 the Crime Writers' Gold Dagger Award for *A Fatal Inversion*, written under the name Barbara Vine.

RUTH
RENDELL

TO FEAR A
PAINTED DEVIL

ARROW BOOKS

Arrow Books Limited
62-65 Chandos Place, London WC2N 4NW

An imprint of Century Hutchinson Limited

London Melbourne Sydney Auckland
Johannesburg and agencies throughout
the world

First published by John Long 1965
Arrow edition 1979
Reprinted 1982, 1984, 1986 and 1988
Reissued 1989

Printed and bound in Great Britain by
Courier International Ltd, Tiptree, Essex

ISBN 0 09 920360 X

For
MARGARET AND CYRIL RABBS
with love

the sleeping and the dead
Are but as pictures: 'tis the eye of childhood
That fears a painted devil.

Macbeth

Prologue

He was nine. It was his first morning in England and he began to wonder if all English houses were like this one, large yet with small rooms, full of things that no one could use: armless statues, vases with lids to them, curtains as immoveably draped as one of his mother's evening gowns.

They had arrived the night before and he had passed through the hall wrapped in a blanket and carried in his father's arms. He remembered only the great front door, a heavy wooden door with a picture of a tree on it in coloured glass. They had left him to sleep as long as he would and someone had brought breakfast for him on a tray. Now as he descended the stairs, crossing the half-landing which a bronze soldier guarded with his lance, he saw the hall below him and his steps faltered.

It was a fine morning but the room looked as rooms do at twilight, dim and still. Instead of being papered the walls were hung with embroideries stretched on frames, and between them curtains that covered—what? Windows? Doors? It seemed to him that they covered things people were not supposed to see. There was a single mirror with a wooden frame and this frame, of carved and polished red wood, looked as if it had grown branches of its own, for strips of wood shaped into leaves and twigs twined across the glass.

Within this mirror he could see not himself but an open door reflected and beyond it the beginning of the garden.

The door stood wide and he went through it, seeking the garden where he knew the sun must be shining. Then he saw the picture. He stood quite still and he stared at it.

It was a painting of a lady in an old-fashioned dress of striped silk, bright blue and gold, with a little gold cap on her head. She was holding a silver plate and in the plate was the head of a man.

He knew it must be a very good painting because the artist had made it look so real. Nothing was left out, not even the blood in the plate and the white tube things in the man's neck where it had been cut from his body.

The lady wasn't looking at the thing in the plate but at him. She was smiling and there was a strange expression on her face, dreamy, triumphant, replete. He had never seen such a look in anyone's eyes before but suddenly he knew with an intuition that had in it something of an *a priori* knowledge, that grown-ups sometimes looked at each other like that and that they did so out of the sight of children.

He tore his eyes from the picture and put his hand up to his mouth to stop them hearing his scream. Then he rushed blindly away, making for the glass place that separated this room from the garden.

He stumbled at the step and put out his hand to save himself. It touched something cool and soft—but only for a moment. The coolness and softness were succeeded by a terrible burning pain that seemed to smite him exactly like the shock he had had from his mother's electric iron.

Away in the garden someone laughed. He screamed and screamed and screamed until he heard doors banging, feet flying, the women coming to him from the kitchen.

PART ONE

1

'PRUSSIC acid?' The chemist was startled. He had been a member of the Pharmaceutical Society for ten years and this was the first time anyone had made such a request to him. Not that he would grant it. He was a responsible citizen, almost—in his own estimation—a doctor. 'Cyanide of Potassium?' He looked severely at the small man in the suit that was too dark and too thick for a hot day. 'What d'you want that for?'

Edward Carnaby, for his part, was affronted. Mr. Waller was only a chemist, a pharmacist really, not a proper chemist who worked in a laboratory. Everyone knew that doctors poked their noses into one's affairs, trying to find out things that were no business of theirs, but not chemists. You asked for what you wanted—razor blades or shaving cream or a camera film—and the chemist gave it to you. He wrapped it up and you paid for it. When all was said and done Waller was only a shopkeeper.

'I want it for killing wasps. I've got a wasp nest on the wall of my house under the roof.'

He fidgeted uneasily under Waller's accusing gaze. The fan on the ceiling, instead of cooling the shop, was only blowing the hot air about.

'May I have your name, please?'

'What for? I don't have to have a prescription for it, do I?'

11

Waller ignored the sarcasm. Responsible professional men must not allow themselves to be ruffled by cheap cracks.

'What gave you the idea of cyanide?' As he spoke the curtain of coloured plastic strips that hung across the entrance to the dispensary parted and Linda Gaveston came out in her pink overall. Her appearance angered Edward, partly because she looked so cool, partly because he felt that a girl whose parents lived on Linchester had no business to be working as an assistant in a chemist's shop. She smiled at him vaguely. Edward snapped:

'If you must know, I read about it in a gardening book.'

Plausible, Waller thought.

'Rather an old-fashioned book, surely? These days we get rid of wasps by using a reliable vespicide.' He paused, allowing the unfamiliar word to sink in. 'One that is harmless to warm-blooded . . .'

'All right,' Edward interrupted him. He wasn't going to make a scene in front of one of those snooty Gavestons. 'Why didn't you say so before? I'll take it. What's it called?'

'Vesprid.' Waller shot him a last baleful look and turned round, but the girl—showing off, Edward thought—was already holding the tin towards him. 'Two and eleven.'

'Thanks,' Edward said shortly, taking the penny change.

'The instructions are enclosed.'

Linda Gaveston lifted her shoulders slightly and slipped between the waving strips in the way she had seen a night club girl insinuate herself through a bead curtain on television.

'There goes a nut,' she said to Waller when Edward had gone. 'He lives near us.'

'Really?' Like all the shopkeepers in Chantflower village Waller had a great respect for Linchester. Money flowed from it as from a spring of sweet water. 'Not quite what one has been led to expect.' He watched Edward get into his salesman's car, its back seat full of cardboard boxes. 'It takes all sorts,' he said.

On that hot afternoon Freda Carnaby was the only Linchester housewife who was really working and she was not a wife at all. She was cleaning the windows in the single living room of Edward's chalet partly because she was houseproud and partly because it was a good excuse for watching the cars coming round The Circle. Linchester business men kept short hours and the man she was looking for might be early. He would wave, even perhaps stop and renew his promise to see her later, and he would notice afresh how efficient she was, how womanly. Moreover he would see that she could look smart and pretty not only in the evenings but also with a wash leather in her hand.

Considering who she was looking for it was ironic that the first car to appear was Tamsin Selby's. Even if you didn't see the number plate (SIN 1A) you would know it was Tamsin's Mini because, although it was new, its black body and white roof were already marked with raindrops and with dust, and the back seat was full of leaves and twigs, rubbish from the fields. Freda pursed her lips in happy disapproval. If you had money and you bought nice things (what that monogram of a number plate must have cost!) you ought to take care of them.

Dr. Greenleaf's car followed fast on her tail. It was time, Freda considered, that he bought a new one. A doctor, she had read in one of her magazines, was nowadays the most respected member of a community, and therefore had appearances to keep up. She smiled and bobbed her head. She thought the doctor's kindly grin meant he was grateful to her for being so healthy and not taking up his surgery time.

By the time Joan Smith-King arrived with her shooting

brake full of the Linchester children she had fetched from school, Freda had finished the window.

'All delivered in plain vans,' Joan said cheerfully. 'Den says I ought to have a C licence.'

'Can I go to tea with Peter?' Cheryl called. 'Can I, Auntie Free? Please.'

'If you're sure she's no trouble,' Freda said. Cheryl might be only a salesman's daughter, but she had nice manners. She, Freda, had seen to that. But going out to tea was a nuisance. Now Cheryl would come rushing in at seven just when Freda wanted to be relaxed and ready with coffee cups on the best traycloth, paper napkins and sherry in a decanter.

'Ghastly these wasps.' Joan looked up at the chalet roof where the wasps were dribbling out from under the eaves. 'Tamsin said Patrick got a nasty sting on his hand.'

'Did he?' Freda took her eyes from Joan's face and stared innocently at the hedge. 'Don't be late,' she said to Cheryl. Joan moved off, one hand on the wheel, the other pulling Jeremy off Peter, shoving her daughter Susan into Cheryl's lap. The baby in its carry-cot on the front seat began to cry. Freda went round the back and into the spotless kitchen.

She was re-doing her face from the little *cache* of cosmetics she kept in a drawer when she heard Edward's car draw up on the drive. The front door slammed.

'Free?'

She bustled into the lounge. Edward was already at the record-player, starting up The Hall of the Mountain King.

'You might have shut the gates,' she said from the window, but she didn't press the point. A wife could expect small services, not a sister. A sister was only a housekeeper, a nanny to Edward's motherless daughter. Still . . . she cheered up. A couple of years and she might have a child of her own.

'How long till tea?'

'Five thirty sharp,' said Freda. 'I'm sure I never keep you waiting for your meals, Ted.'

'Only it's car maintenance at seven.'

Edward went to a different class each night. French on Mondays and Thursdays, accountancy on Tuesdays, carpentry on Wednesdays, car maintenance on Fridays. Freda approved his industry. It was a way, she supposed, of forgetting the wife who had lived just long enough to put the curtains up in the new house and who had died before the first instalment was due on the mortgage.

'What are you going to do?'

She shrugged. He was her brother, but he was also her twin and as jealous of her time as a husband might be.

'Sometimes,' he said, 'I wonder if you haven't got a secret boy-friend who pops in when I'm out of the way.'

Had there been talk, gossip? Well, why not? Only a few days now and everyone would know. Edward would know. Funny, but it made her shiver to think of it.

He turned the record over and straightened up. Solveig's Song, music for a cold climate, soared into the stuffy room. The pure voice pleased Freda, reminding her of large uncluttered rooms she had so far seen only from the outside as she passed with her shopping baskets. On the whole, she thought, she would like to live there. She wouldn't be squeamish. He loves me, she thought, not thinking of Edward. A long shudder of pain and anxious happiness travelled down from her shoulders and along her thighs to her feet in their tight pointed shoes.

'I wouldn't like that, Free,' he said. 'You're best off here with me.'

'We shall have to see what time brings forth, shan't we?' she said, staring through the diamond panes at Linchester, at ten more houses that encircled a green plot. How nice, how stimulating it would be next year to see it all from a different angle. When she turned round Edward was beside her, flicking his fingers in front of her face to break up the myopic stare.

'Don't,' she said. Hurt, he sat down and opened his homework book, *An Outline of Monetary Economics*. Freda went upstairs to lacquer her hair, straighten her stocking seams and spray a little more Fresh Mist under her arms.

Denholm Smith-King was used to performing small and, for that matter, large services for his wife. With five children he could hardly do otherwise. He was already at home when she arrived back, making what he called euphemistically 'a cup of tea'. In the Smith-King household this meant slicing and buttering a whole large loaf and carving up a couple of pound cakes.

'You're early,' she said.

'Not much doing.' He greeted Cheryl vaguely as if he was uncertain whether or not she was one of his own children. 'Things are a bit slack so I hied me to the bosom of my family.'

'Slack?' She found a tablecloth and spread it on what had once been a fine unblemished sheet of teak. 'I don't like the sound of that, Den. I'm always meaning to talk to you about the business. . . .'

'Did you find anyone to sit in with the mob tomorrow night?' he asked, adroitly changing the subject.

'Linda Gaveston said she'd come. I asked her when I was in Waller's.' Joan found the piece of pasteboard from the mêlée on the mantelpiece and read its message aloud: 'Tamsin and Patrick Selby At Home. Saturday, July 4th, eight p.m. Of course I know how affected Tamsin is, but At Home's going a bit far.'

'I reckon you can go as far as you like,' said Denholm, 'when you've got a private income and no kids.'

'It's only a birthday party. She's twenty-seven tomorrow.'

Denholm sat down heavily, a reluctant paterfamilias at the head of his table. 'Twenty-seven? I wouldn't have put her at a day over twenty.'

'Oh, don't be so silly, Den. They've been married for years.' She had been piqued by his admiration of another woman, but now she looked at him tenderly over their children's heads. 'Fancy being married for years to Patrick Selby!'

'I daresay it's all a matter of taste, old girl.'

'I don't know what it is,' Joan said, 'but he frightens me. I get the shivers every time I see him walking past here with that great German dog of his.' She wiped the baby's chin and sighed. 'It came in the garden again this morning. Tamsin was most apologetic. I'll grant her that. She's a nice enough girl in her way, only she always seems only half awake.'

'Pity they haven't got any kids,' Denholm said wistfully. Uncertain as to whether he was wishing children on to the Selbys from genuine regret for their childlessness or from motives of revenge, Joan gave him a sharp look.

'They're first cousins, you know.'

'Ah,' said Denholm, 'brought up together. One of those boy and girl things, was it?'

'I don't know,' said his wife. 'He's not likely to confide in anyone and she's far too much of the little girl lost.'

When tea was over the children drifted into the garden. Joan handed her husband a tea towel and began to wash up. Jeremy's scream made them both jump and before it had died away Denholm, who knew what it meant, was out on the lawn brandishing the stick he kept in the storm porch for this purpose.

Only Cheryl had not backed away. The other children clung to Denholm as he advanced between the swing and the sandpit.

'Get out of it, you great brute!'

The Weimaraner looked at him courteously but with a kind of mild disdain. There was nothing savage about her but nothing endearing either. She was too autocratic, too highly-bred for that. Haunch-deep in marigolds, she was standing in the middle of Denholm's herbaceous border and now, as he shouted at her again, she flicked out a raspberry pink tongue and delicately snapped off a larkspur blossom.

Cheryl caught at Denholm's hand. 'She's a nice dog, really she is. She often comes to our house.'

Her words meant nothing to Denholm but he dropped the stick. Insensitive as he was, he could hardly beat the dog in the presence of the woman who had appeared so suddenly and so silently on the lawn next door.

'Queenie often comes to our house,' Cheryl said again.

Tamsin Selby had heard. A spasm of pain crossed her smooth brown face and was gone.

'I'm so dreadfully sorry.' She smiled without showing her teeth. 'Please don't be cross, Denholm. She's very gentle.'

Denholm grinned foolishly. The Selbys, both of them, always made him feel a fool. It was the contrast, perhaps, between their immaculate garden and his own cluttered playground; their pale hand-stitched clothes and what he called his 'togs'; their affluence and his need.

'It puts the wind up the youngsters,' he said gruffly.

'Come on, Queenie!' The long brown arm rose languidly in an elegant parabola. At once the dog leaped, clearing the hedge with two inches to spare. 'I hope we'll see you tomorrow, Denholm?'

'You can count on us. Never miss a good booze-up.' He was embarrassed and he went in quickly. But Cheryl lingered, staring over the hedge with curious intelligent eyes and wondering why the lady who was so unlike Auntie Free had fallen to her knees under the willow tree and flung her arms round the dog's creamy sable neck.

2

FIVE years before when Nottinghamshire people talked about Linchester they meant the Manor and the park. If they were county they remembered garden parties, if not, coach trips to a Palladian house where you paid half-a-crown to look at a lot of valuable but boring china while the children rolled down the ha-ha. But all that came to an end when old Marvell died. One day, it seemed, the Manor was there, the next there were just the bulldozers Henry Glide brought over from the city and a great cloud of dust floating above the trees, grey and pancake-shaped, as if someone had exploded a small atom bomb.

Nobody would live there, they said, forgetting that commuting was the fashion even in the provinces. Henry himself had his doubts and he had put up three chalet bungalows before he realised he might be on to a better thing if he forgot all about retired farmers and concentrated on Nottingham company directors. Fortunately, but by the merest chance, the three mistakes were almost hidden by a screen of elms. He nearly lost his head and built big houses with small gardens all over the estate, but he had a cautious look at the Marvell contract and saw that there was an embargo on too much tree-felling. His wife thought he was getting senile when he said he was only going to put up eight more houses, eight beautiful architect-designed houses around a broad green plot with a pond in the middle.

And that was what people meant now when they talked about Linchester. They meant The Green with the pond where swans glided between lily leaves as big as dinner plates; The Circle which was a smart name for the road that ran around The Green; the Cotswold farmhouse and the mock-Tudor lodge, the Greenleafs' place that might have been prefabricated in Hampstead Garden Suburb and flown complete into Nottinghamshire, the Selbys' glass box and Glide's own suntrap bungalow. They pointed from the tops of buses on the Nottingham road at the Gavestons' pocket-sized grange, the Gages' Queen Anne and the Smith-King place that had started off as a house and now was just a breeding box. They criticised the chalets, those poor relations and their occupants, the Staxtons, the Macdonalds and the Carnabys.

The two men in the British Railways lorry lived in Newark and they had never been to Linchester before. Now, on the calmest, most beautiful evening of the summer, they saw it at its best. Yet it was not the loveliness of the place that impressed them, the elegant sweep of The Circle, the stone pineapples on the pillars at the Manor gates, nor the trees, elms, oaks and sycamores, that gave each house its expensive privacy, but the houses themselves and their opulence.

Over-awed and at the same time suspicious, they drove between the pillars and into The Circle itself, looking for a house called Hallows.

The lorry rumbled along the road, making ruts in the melting tar and sending white spar chips flying, past the three mistakes, past Shalom, The Laurels, Linchester Lodge.

'That's the one I'd fancy,' said the driver, pointing to the Cotswold farmhouse with a hint of Swiss chalet in its jade-coloured balconies. 'If my pools come up.' His mate was silent, consumed with envy and with scorn.

'Keep your eyes open, Reg. It's gone knocking-off time.'

'Blimey,' said his mate, throwing his cigarette end into the Gavestons' rhododendrons, 'I haven't got X-ray eyes. It's half a mile up to them front doors, and what with the trees.'

'Now, I'd have them down. Keep out the light, they do. And I'd do something about that empty bit in the middle. You could put up a couple of nice bungalows where that pond is. Here we are. Hallows. I don't know what I brought you for. I could have done better on my tod.'

But he was glad of Reg's help when it came to unloading the parcel. It was heavy and, according to the label, fragile. Something like a door it was or a big mirror. He could just feel a frame thing through the corrugated cardboard.

They humped it up the drive between two rows of young willows until they came to the paved court in front of the house.

Hallows was beautiful—by most people's standards. Reg and the driver found it on the dull side compared with its ornate neighbours. This house was plain and rectangular, built of York stone and pale unpolished wood; there were no gables and no chimneys, no shutters and not a single pane of stained glass. The windows were huge, backed with white venetian blinds, and the front doors were swing affairs of glass set in steel.

'Are you looking for me?' The voice, delicate, vague, unmistakeably upper-class, came from above their heads. The driver looked up to a long undecorated balcony and saw a woman leaning over the rails.

'British Railways, lady.'

'Too dreadful! ' Tamsin Selby said. 'I'd forgotten all about it.'

It was true, she had. The delivery of this parcel had been planned in a sprightly, almost malicious mood, very different from her present one. But it had taken so long in coming, so much had happened. She disappeared through the balcony windows back into the bedroom.

'How the rich live,' Reg said to the driver. 'Forgotten, my foot!'

Tamsin came out to them breathlessly. At all costs it must be got in and, if possible, hidden, before Patrick came home. She tried to take it from them but the weight was too much for her. The men watched her efforts with a kind of triumph.

'Would you be terribly sweet,' Tamsin said, 'and carry it upstairs for me?'

'Now, look,' the driver began, 'it's heavy . . .'

She took two half-crowns from the bag she had snatched up in the hall.

'Can't leave it here, can we?' Reg was grinning reluctantly.

'So kind,' said Tamsin. She led the way and they followed her, carrying the parcel gingerly to avoid scraping the dove-grey hessian on the hall walls, the paint on the curled iron baluster rails.

'In here, I think.'

The room was too beautiful for them. Poverty, never admitted, scarcely felt before, scummed their hands with ineluctable dirt. They looked away from the velvet curtains, the dressing-table glass ringed with light bulbs, the half-open door that showed a glimpse of a shower cabinet and tiles hand-painted with fishes, and down at their own feet.

'Could you put it on one of the beds?'

They lowered it on to the nearer of the cream silk counterpanes, avoiding the bed by the window where the turned-back cover revealed a lemon lace nightgown folded between frilled nylon pillow and frilled nylon sheet.

'Thank you so much. It won't be in the way here.'

She didn't even bother to smooth the silk where a corner of the parcel had ruffled it, but signed her name quickly and hustled them out of the house. After they had gone she closed the spare bedroom door and sighed deeply. Patrick would be home any minute now and she had meant to use those spare moments checking on everything, making sure she looked her best.

She went into the bedroom with the balcony and looked at herself in the glass. That was all right, just the way Patrick liked her to look, the way he had liked her to look once . . . The sun—she had spent most of the day in the sun—had done wonders for her already brown skin and had faintly bleached her dark honey hair. No make-up. To have put on lipstick would have been to spoil the image she liked to create, the facsimile of a smooth teak-coloured mask, straight nose, carved lips, cheekbones that were arched polished planes.

Her hair hung quite straight on to her brown shoulders. Even for him she refused to cut it short and have it set. The dress—that was all right at any rate. Patrick hated bright colours and this one was black and white. Plain as it was, she knew there might be something too casual about it, too suggestive of a uniform for emancipated women. O God, she thought, making a face at her own image and wishing for the first time in her life that it could be transmuted into the reflection of a brisk blonde *hausfrau*.

Downstairs the table was already laid for dinner: two place mats of blue linen—he had made her give up using the big damask cloths—black Prinknash plates, a long basket of French bread, Riesling dewed from the refrigerator. Tamsin gasped aloud when she saw that she had forgotten to throw away the vaseful of grasses. She grabbed them, scattering brown seeds, and rushed to the kitchen. The dog now, had she fed the dog?

'Queenie!'

How many times in the past months had he scolded her

for failing to feed the dog on the dot of five? How many times had he snapped at her for wasting her days dreaming in the garden and the fields, learning country lore from Crispin Marvell, when she should have been at home keeping up with the Gages and the Gavestons.

But she must have done it and, in her panic, forgotten all about it. The plate of congealing horsemeat and biscuit meal was still on the floor, untouched by the dog. Flies buzzed over it and a single wasp crawled across a chunk of fat.

'Queenie!'

The bitch appeared silently from the garden door, sniffed at the food and looked enquiringly at Tamsin with mournful eyes. She is the only thing that we have together now, Tamsin thought, the only thing that we both love, Kreuznacht Konigin, that we both call Queenie. She dropped to her knees and in her loneliness she put her arms round Queenie's neck, feeling the suede-smooth skin against her own cheek. Queenie's tail flapped and she nuzzled against Tamsin's ear.

Of the two female creatures desirous of pleasing Patrick it was the dog who heard him first. She stiffened and the swinging lethargic tail began to wag excitedly, banging against the cooker door and making a noise like a gong.

'Master,' Tamsin said. 'Go, find him!'

The Weimaraner stretched her lean body, cocked her head and stood for a moment poised, much as her ancestors had done listening for the huntsman's command in the woods of Thuringia a century ago. The heavy garage door rumbled and fell with a faint clang. Queenie was away, across the patio, leaping for the iron gate that shut off the drive.

Tamsin followed, her heart pounding.

He came in slowly, not looking at her, silent, his attention given solely to the dog. When he had fondled Queenie, his hands drawing down the length of her body, he looked up and saw his wife.

Tamsin had so much to say, so many endearments remembered from the days when it was necessary to say nothing. No words came. She stood there, looking at him, her hands kneading the black and white stuff of her dress. Swinging the ignition key, Patrick pushed past her, shied at a wasp that dived against his face, and went into the house.

'She hasn't eaten her dinner,' were the first words that he spoke to her. He hated dirt, disorder, matter in the wrong place. 'It's all over flies.'

Tamsin picked up the plate and dropped the contents into the waste disposal unit. Meat juice rubbed off on to her fingers. Patrick looked pointedly at her hand, turned and went upstairs. She ran the tap, rinsed her fingers. It seemed an age since he had gone—the wine, would it get too warm? Ought she to put it back in the fridge? She waited, the sweat seeping into her dress. Presently she switched on the fan.

At last he came in wearing terylene slacks and a tee shirt of pale striped cotton, and he looked handsome if you admired men with ash-blond hair and freckles so dense that they looked like tan.

'I thought you'd like melon,' she said. 'It's canteloupe.'

Suspiciously Patrick skimmed away the melting golden sugar.

'Not honey, is it? You know I hate honey.'

'Of course it isn't.' She paused timidly. 'Darling,' she said.

He made his way silently through chicken salad, potato sticks, fruit salad (all good hygienic food from tins and packets and deep freezers), eating sparingly, absent-mindedly. The fan whirred and Queenie lay beneath it, paws spread, tongue extended.

'I've got everything in for the party,' Tamsin said.

'Party?'

'Tomorrow. It's my birthday. You hadn't forgotten?'

'No, it slipped my mind, that's all.'

Had it also slipped his mind to get her a present?

'There's heaps to do,' she said brightly. 'The lights to put up, and we've got to move the furniture in the—' Now it was more than ever important to pick the right word, '—the lounge in case it rains. And—Oh, Patrick, could you do something about the wasps? I'm sure there's a nest somewhere.' She remembered belatedly and reached for his hand. The fingers lay inert in hers, the big red swelling showing at the base of his thumb. 'Too frightful for you. How's it been today?'

'The sting? Oh, all right. It's going down.'

'Could you possibly try to get rid of them? They'll ruin the party.'

He pushed away his plate and his half-finished glass of wine.

'Not tonight. I'm going out.'

She had begun to tremble and when she spoke her voice shook.

'There's so much to do. Please don't go, darling. I need you.'

Patrick laughed. She didn't look at him but sat staring at her plate, moving the viscous yellow juice about with her spoon.

'I *am* going out. I have to take the dog, don't I?'

'I'll take the dog.'

'Thank you very much,' he said icily. 'I can manage.' He touched the venetian blind and glanced at the faint patina of dust on his fingertips. 'If you're bored there are things here which could do with some attention.'

27

'Patrick.' Her face had paled and there were goose pimples on her arms. 'About what you said last night—you've got to change your mind. You've got to forget all about it ' With a great effort she pushed three words from stiff lips: 'I love you.'

She might not have spoken. He walked into the kitchen and took the leash from the broom cupboard.

'Queenie! '

From deep sleep the Weimaraner galvanised into impassioned life. Patrick fastened the steel clip to her collar and led her out through the french windows.

Tamsin sat among the ruins of her meal. Presently she began to cry silently, the tears splashing into the wine glass she held in her cupped hands. Her mouth was dry and she drank. I am drinking my own sorrow, she thought. Five minutes, ten minutes passed. Then she went to the front door and out into the willow avenue. The sky was clear, azure above, violet and apricot on the horizon, thronged with wheeling swallows.

She stopped at the end of the drive and leaned on the gate. Patrick hadn't gone far. She could see him standing with his back to her on The Green staring down at the waters of the pond. The dog had tried, unsuccessfully as always, to intimidate the three white swans. Now she had given up and was following a squirrel trail, pausing at the foot of each tree and peering up into the branches. Patrick was waiting for something, whiling away his time. For what?

As she watched him, a pale green Ford swung into view from behind the elms. That funny little salesman fellow from the chalets, she thought, on his way to his evening class. She hoped he'd pass on with a wave but he didn't. He stopped. Few men passed Tamsin Selby without a second glance.

'Hot enough for you?'

'I like it,' Tamsin said. What was his name? Only one chalet dweller was known to her by name. 'I love the sun.'

'Ah well, it suits you. I can see that.'

Conversation would have to be made. She opened the gate and went over to the car. He mistook her action and opened the door.

'Can I give you a lift? I'm going to the village.'

'No. No, thanks.' Tamsin almost laughed. 'I'm not going out. Just enjoying the evening.'

His face fell.

'As a matter of fact,' he said, stalling, trying to keep her with him long enough for the neighbours to see him talking to the beautiful Mrs. Selby, 'as a matter of fact I'm playing truant. Supposed to be doing a little job exterminating pests.'

'Pests?'

'Wasps. We've got a nest.'

'Have you? So have we.' She looked up. Patrick was still there. 'My husband—we want to get rid of them but we don't know how.'

'I've got some stuff. It's called Vesprid. I tell you what. When I've done mine I'll bring the tin round. There's bags of it, enough to kill all the wasps in Nottinghamshire.'

'But how kind!'

'I'll bring it round in the morning, shall I?'

Tamsin sighed. Now she would have to have this wretched man in the way while she was preparing for the party.

'Look, why don't you come to a little do I'm having, a few friends in for drinks at about eight?' He looked at her adoringly and his eyes reminded her of Queenie's. 'If you could come early we could do the wasps then. Bring a friend if you like.'

A party at Hallows! A party at the biggest house on Linchester! Putting on his maudlin widower's voice, he said: 'I haven't been to a party since I lost my wife.'

'Really?' A chord had been struck. 'His wife's dead,' Patrick had said, 'and that's why . . .' What had she done? 'I'm sorry but I don't think I know your name.'

'Carnaby. Edward Carnaby.'

He looked at her, smiling. She took her hand from the car door and pressed it against her breastbone, breathing like one who has run up a steep hill.

Trust Tamsin Selby to be talking to a man, Joan thought, as she came out of her gate, holding Cheryl by the hand.

'Wave to your Daddy.'

The child was more interested in the man and the dog on The Green. Telling herself that she had meant to go that way in any case, Joan followed her reluctantly.

Patrick had never been one to waste words on the weather or other people's health. His eyes, which had been fixed with a kind of calculating disgust on Edward Carnaby, now turned upon Joan, taking in the details of her limp cotton dress, her sunburned arms and the brown roots of her hair where the rinse was growing out.

'Isn't it *hot*?' She was uncomfortable in his presence and felt the remark had been foolish. In fact, it was no longer particularly hot. A faint breeze was stirring the waters of the pond, ruffling it to match the mackerel sky.

'I don't know why English people make a cult of grumbling about the weather,' he said. He looked very Teutonic as he spoke and she remembered someone had told her he had spent his childhood in Germany and America. She laughed awkwardly and made a grab for Cheryl's hand. He had made it so clear he didn't want to talk to her that she jumped and blushed when he called her back.

30

'How's business?'

'Business?' Of course he meant Denholm's business, the factory. 'All right, I suppose,' she said, and then because ever since before tea there had been a vague, half-formed worry nagging at her mind, 'Den says things have been a bit slack lately.'

'We can't all get Harwell contracts.' He touched the trunk of a great oak and with a small smile looked up into its branches. 'They don't grow on trees. It's a matter of work, my dear Joan, work and single-mindedness. Denholm will have to watch his step or I'll be taking him over one of these days.'

She said nothing. Malice quirked the corners of his thin mouth. She looked away from him and at the dog. Then she saw that he, too, was staring in the same direction.

'Expansion is life,' he said. 'Give it a few months and then we'll make things hum.'

Shivering a little, she drew back from him, feeling a sudden chill that seemed to come not from the scurrying wind but from the man himself.

'We're late, Cheryl. It's past your bedtime.'

'She can come with me,' said Patrick, his curious smile broadening. 'I'm going that way.'

The green Ford had moved away from the Hallows gate but Tamsin was still there, watching. As the man and child walked off towards the chalets, Joan suddenly thought she would go and speak to Tamsin, demand the explanation she knew Patrick would never give to her. But Tamsin, she saw, was in no mood for talking. Something or someone had upset her and she was retreating up the willow drive, her head bent and her hands clenched beneath her chin. Joan went home and put the children to bed. When she came downstairs Denholm was asleep. He looked so like Jeremy,

31

his eyes lightly closed, his cheek pink and smooth against the bunched-up cushion, that she hadn't the heart to wake him.

Edward Carnaby kept on turning back and waving all the way down to the Manor gates. Tamsin stared after him, unable to smile in return. Her knees felt weak and she was afraid she might faint. When she reached the house she heard Queenie bark, a single staccato bark followed by a howl. The howls went on for a few seconds; then they stopped and all was silent. Tasmin knew what the howls meant. Patrick had tied up the dog to go into someone's house.

She went upstairs and into the balcony room. In the faint bloom on the dressing-table Patrick had written with a precise finger: Dust this. She fell on the bed and lay face-downwards.

Half an hour had passed when she heard the footsteps and at first she thought they were Patrick's. But whoever it was was coming alone. There was no accompanying tip-tap of dog's claws on stone. O God, she thought, I shall have to tell him. Otherwise Patrick might, there in front of everyone at the party.

The doors were unlocked. There was nothing to stop him coming in, but he didn't. He knocked with the prearranged signal. What would he do when he knew it all? There was still a chance she could persuade Patrick. She put her fingers in her ears, willing him to go. He knocked again and it seemed to her that he must hear through glass and wood, stone walls and thick carpets, the beating of her heart.

At last he went away.

'Damnation!' she heard him say from beneath her as if he were looking through the lounge window. The footsteps hurried away down the avenue and out through the footpath on to the Nottingham road. The gate swung, failed to catch and flapped against the post, bang, swing, bang. Tamsin went into the room where the men had put the parcel. She broke her nails untying the string but she was crying too much to notice.

3

THERE are perhaps few things more galling to one's *amour propre* than to act in a covert, clandestine way when no such discretion is necessary. Oliver Gage was a proud man and now, creeping round the Hallows paths, tapping signals on the glass doors, he felt that someone had made a fool of him.

'Damnation!' he said, this time under his breath.

She had obviously gone out with *him*. Pressure had been put on her. Well, so much the better if that meant she had been preparing the ground. He would make his intentions clear at the party.

He went out into The Circle and made the humiliating detour necessary before he could find his car that he had parked on the ride off the main road. When he entered Linchester for the second time that night it was by the Manor gates and he drove into his own garage drive with a sense of disgruntled virtue and the shame he always felt when he returned to his house. Oliver lived in one of the largest houses on Linchester but it was too small for him. He hated it already. Every Friday night when he came up from his four days in London the sight of the house, magnified perhaps in his mind during his absence, sickened him and reminded him afresh of his misfortunes. For, as Oliver grew older, the sizes of his houses diminished. This was not due to a reversal in his financial life. One of the executives of a national daily, his income now topped the seven thousand mark, but only about a third of this found its way into Oliver's pocket. The rest, never seen by him yet never forgotten, streamed away via an army of solicitors and bank managers and accountants into the laps of his two discarded wives.

When he had married Nancy—pretty, witty Nancy! —and built this, the smallest of his houses to date, he had forgotten for a few months the other pressures on his income. Was not love a Hercules, still climbing trees in the Hesperides? Now, a year later, he reflected that the gods were just and of his pleasant vices had made instruments to plague him.

He unlocked the door and dropped his keys on to the hall table between the Flamenco doll and the cherry heering bottle that Nancy by the addition of a shade stuck all over with hotel labels had converted into a lamp. In all his matrimonial career Oliver had never before given houseroom to such an object. He hated it but he felt that, in ensuring it was the first thing his eye fell on when he entered his home, Providence was meting out to him a stern exquisite justice.

Nancy's sewing machine could be heard faintly from the lounge. The querulous whine of the motor fanned his ill-temper into rage. He pushed open the reeded glass door and went in. The room was tightly sealed and stifling, the windows all closed and the curtains drawn back in the way he loathed, carelessly, with no attention to the proper arrangement of their folds. Those curtains had cost him thirty pounds.

His wife—to himself and to one other Oliver occasionally referred to her as his present wife—lifted her foot from the pedal which controlled the motor and pushed damp hair back from a face on which sweat shone. Shreds of cotton and pieces of coloured fluff clung to her dress and littered the floor. There was even a piece of cotton dangling from her bracelet.

'My Christ, it's like an oven in here!' Oliver flung back the french windows and scowled at Bernice Greenleaf who was walking coolly about the garden next-door, snipping the dead blossoms off an opulent Zephirine Drouhin. When she waved to him he changed the scowl into a rigid smirk 'What in God's name are you doing?' he asked his wife.

She pulled a cobbled strip of black and red silk from under the needle. 'I'm making a dress for Tamsin's party.'

Oliver sat down heavily, catching his foot in one of the Numdah rugs. ('If we have wood block flooring and rugs, darling,' Nancy had said, 'we'll save pounds on carpeting.')

'This I cannot understand,' Oliver said. 'Did I or did I not give you a cheque for twenty pounds last Tuesday with express instructions to buy yourself a dress?'

'Well . . .'

'Did I or did I not? That's all I ask. It's a perfectly simple question.'

Nancy's babyish, *gamine* face puckered. A curly face, he had called it once, tenderly, lovingly, touching with a teasing finger the tip-tilted nose, the bunchy cheeks, the fluffy fair eyebrows.

'Well, darling, I had to have shoes, you see, and stockings. And there was the milk bill . . .' Her voice faltered. 'I saw this remnant and this pattern . . .' She held an envelope towards him diffidently. Oliver glowered at the coloured picture of three improbably tall women in cylindrical cotton frocks. 'It'll be all right, won't it?'

'It will be quite ghastly,' Oliver said coldly. 'I shall be covered with shame. I shall be mortified. Tamsin always looks wonderful.'

As soon as the words were out he regretted them. Now

36

was not the time. Nancy was going to cry. Her face swelled as if the skin itself was allergic to his anger.

'Tamsin has a private income.' The tears spouted. 'I only wanted to save you money. That's all I think about, saving your money.'

'Oh, don't cry! I'm sorry, Nancy.' She almost fell from her chair into his lap and he put his arms round her with the distaste that was part of his marital experience, the distaste that always came as love ebbed. Every bit of her was damp and clinging and unbearably hot.

'I do want to economise, darling. I keep thinking of all that money going out month after month to Jean and Shirley. And what with both the boys at Bembridge . . .' Oliver frowned. He disliked the reminder that he had been unable to afford to send the sons of his first marriage to Marlborough. 'And Shirley always so greedy, insisting on sending Jennifer to a private school when state education is so good these days.'

'You know nothing at all about state education,' Oliver said.

'Oh, darling, why did you have to marry such unattractive women? Any other women would have got married again. Two such disastrous—well, tragic marriages. I lie awake at night thinking about the inroads on our income.'

She was off on a well-worn track, the Friday night special. Oliver let her talk, reaching to the mantelpiece for a cigarette from the box.

'And I haven't got anything exciting for your dinner,' she finished on a note of near-triumph.

'We'll go out to eat, then.'

'You know we can't afford it. Besides I've got to finish this filthy dress.' She struggled from his lap back to the sewing machine.

'This,' said Oliver, 'is the end.' Nancy, already involved

once more in fitting a huge sleeve into a tiny armhole, ignored him. She was not to know that it was with these words that Oliver had terminated each of his previous marriages. For him, too, they sounded dreadfully like the mere echoes of happy finalities. Must Nancy be his till death parted them? More securely than any devout Catholic, any puritan idealist, he had thought himself until recently, bound to his wife. Hercules had climbed his last tree. Unless—unless things would work out and he could get a wife with money of her own, a beautiful, well-dowered wife . . .

He stepped across the rugs, those small and far from luxuriant oases in the big desert of polished floor, and poured himself a carefully-measured drink. Then he sat down and gazed at their reflections, his and Nancy's, in the glass on the opposite wall. Her remarks as to the unattractiveness of his former wives had seemed to denigrate his own taste and perhaps even his own personal appearance. But now, as he looked at himself, he felt their injustice. Anyone coming in, any stranger would, he thought bitterly, have taken Nancy for the cleaning woman doing a bit of overtime sewing, her hair separated into rough hanks, her face greasy with heat and effort. But as for him, with his smooth dark head, the sharply cut yet sensitive features, the long hands that held the blood-red glass . . . the truth of it was that he was wasted in these provincial, incongruous surroundings.

Nancy got up, shook her hair, and began to pull her dress over her head. She was simply going to try on the limp half-finished thing but Oliver was no fool and he could tell from the way she moved, slowly, coquettishly, that there was also intention to tempt him.

'If you must strip in the living room you might pull the curtains,' he said.

He got up and put his hand to the cords that worked the

38

pulley, first the french windows, then at the long Georgian sashes at the front of the house. The silk folds moved to meet each other but not before, through the strip of narrowing glass, he had seen walking past the gate, a tall fair man who rested a freckled hand on a dog's head, a man who was strolling home to a beautiful well-dowered wife . . .

With this glimpse there came into his mind a sudden passionate wish that this time things might for once go smoothly and to the advantage of Oliver Gage. He stood for a moment, thinking and planning, and then he realised that he had no wish to be here like this in the darkness with his wife, and he reached quickly for the light switch.

It was fully dark, outside as well as in, when Denholm awoke. He blinked, passed his hands across his face and stretched.

'Ah, well,' he said to his wife, 'up the wooden hill.'

She had meant to save it all for the morning, but the hours of sitting silently beside the sleeping man had told on her nerves. His expression became incredulous as she began to tell him of the meeting on The Green.

'He was pulling your leg,' he said.

'No, he wasn't. I wouldn't have believed him only I know you've been worried lately. You have been worried, haven't you?'

'Well, if you must know, things have been a bit dicey.' She listened as the bantering tone left his voice. 'Somebody's been building up a big stake in the company.' Only when he was talking business could Denholm shed facetiousness and become a man instead of a clown. 'It's been done through a nominee and we don't know who it is.'

'But, Den,' she cried, 'that must be Patrick!'

'He wouldn't be interested in us. Selbys are glass, nothing but glass and we're chemicals.'

'He would. I tell you, he is. He's got that contract and he means to expand, to take you over. And it does rest with him. The others are just—what do you call it?—sleeping partners.'

She would have to say it, put into words the grotesque fear that had been churning her thoughts the entire evening.

'D'you know what I think? I think it's all malice, just because you once hit that dog.'

The shot had gone home, but still he hesitated, the jovial man, the confident provider.

'You're a proper old worry-guts, aren't you?' His hand reached for hers and the fingers were cold and not quite steady. 'You don't understand business. Business men don't carry on that way.'

Did they? he wondered. Would they? His own holding in the firm had decreased precariously as his family had increased. How far could he trust the loyalty of those Smith-King uncles and cousins? Would they sell if they were sufficiently tempted?

'I understand people,' Joan said, 'and I understand you. You're not well, Den. The strain's too much for you. I wish you'd see Dr. Greenleaf.'

'I will,' Denholm promised. As he spoke he felt again the vague indefinable pains he had been experiencing lately, the continual malaise. 'I'll have a quiet natter to him tomorrow at the party.'

'I don't want to go.'

Denholm did. Even if it was cold and there wasn't enough to drink, even if they made him dance, it would be wonderful just to get away for one evening from baby-feeding at ten, from Susan who had to have a story and from Jeremy who never slept at all until eleven.

'But we've got a sitter,' he said and he sighed as from above he heard his son's voice calling for a drink of water.

40

Joan went to the door. 'You'll have to talk to Patrick. Oh, I wish we didn't have to go.' She went upstairs with the glass and came down again with the baby in her arms.

Trying to console her, Denholm said weakly, 'Cheer up, old girl. It'll be all right on the night.'

4

WHEN he had been married to Jean, when indeed he had been married to Shirley, he had always been able to pay a man to clean the car. Now he had to do it himself, to stand on the gravel like any twenty-five pound a week commuter, squelching a Woolworth sponge over a car that he was ashamed to be seen driving into the office underground car park. There was, however, one thing about this morning slopping to be thankful for. Since he was outside he had been able to catch the postman and take the letters himself. With a damp hand he felt the letter in his pocket, the letter that had just come from his second wife. There was no reason why Nancy should see it and have cause to moan at him because of its contents. Those begging letters were a continual thorn in his flesh. Why should his daughter go on holiday to Majorca when he could only manage Worthing? Such a wonderful chance for her, Oliver, but of course she, Shirley, couldn't afford the air fare or equip Jennifer with a suitable wardrobe for a seven-year-old in the Balearics. Fifty pounds or perhaps seventy would help. After all, Jennifer was his daughter as well as hers and she was his affectionately, Shirley.

He dropped the sponge into the bucket and bent down to polish the windscreen. Over the hedge he saw that his neighbour was opening his own garage doors, but although he liked the doctor he was in no mood for conversation that

morning. Resentment caught at his throat like heartburn. Greenleaf was wearing another new suit! Gossip had it that the doctor was awaiting delivery of another new car. Oliver could hardly bear it when he compared what he thought of as the doctor's miserable continental medical degree with his own Double First.

'Good morning.'

Greenleaf's car drew level with his own and Oliver was forced to look up into his neighbour's brown, aquiline face. It was a very un-English face, almost Oriental, with dark, close-set eyes, a large intelligent mouth and thick hair, crinkly like that of some ancient Assyrian.

'Oh, hallo,' Oliver said ungraciously. He stood up, making an effort to say something neighbourly, when Nancy came running down the path from the kitchen door. She stopped as she saw the doctor and smiled winningly.

'Off on your rounds? What a pity to have to work on a Saturday! I always tell Oliver he doesn't know his luck, having all these long week-ends.'

Oliver coughed. His other wives had learned that his coughs were pregnant with significance. In Nancy's case there had hardly been time to teach her, and now . . .

'I hope I'll see you tonight,' said the doctor as he began to move off.

'Oh, yes, tonight . . .' Nancy's face had taken on its former lines of displeasure. When Greenleaf was out of earshot she turned sharply to her husband. 'I thought you said you left Tamsin's present on the sideboard.'

Oliver had a nose for a scene. He picked up the bucket and started towards the house.

'I did.'

'You bought that for Tamsin?' She scuttled after him into the dining-room and picked up the scent bottle with its cut-glass stopper. 'Nuit de Beltane? I never heard of such extravagance!'

Oliver could see from the open magazine on the table that she had already been checking the price.

'There you are.' Her finger stabbed at a coloured photograph of a similar bottle. 'Thirty-seven and six!' She slammed the magazine shut and threw it on the floor. 'You must be mad.'

'You can't go to a birthday party empty-handed,' Oliver said weakly. If only he knew for certain. There might, after all, be no point in bothering to keep Nancy sweet. He watched her remove the stopper, sniff the scent and dab a spot on her wrist. While she waved her wrist in front of her nose, inhaling crossly, he washed his hands and closed the back door.

'A box of chocolates would have done.' Nancy said. She lugged the sewing machine up on its rubber mat. 'I mean, it's fantastic spending thirty-seven and six on scent for Tamsin when I haven't even got a decent dress to go in.'

'Oh my God!'

'You don't seem to have a sense of proportion where money's concerned.'

'Keep the scent for God's sake and I'll get some chocolates in the village.'

Immediately she was in his arms. Oliver crushed the letter down more firmly in his pocket.

'Can I really, darling? You are an angel. Only you won't be able to get anything nice in the village. You'll have to nip into Nottingham.'

Disengaging himself, Oliver reflected on his wife's economies. Now there would be the petrol into Nottingham, at least twelve and six for chocolates and he'd still spent nearly two pounds on Nuit de Beltane.

44

Nancy began to sew. The dress had begun to look passable. At least he wouldn't be utterly disgraced.

'Can I come in?'

The voice was Edith Gaveston's. Quick as a flash Nancy ripped the silk from the machine, rolled up the dress and crammed it under a sofa cushion.

'Come in, Edith.'

'I see you've got into our country way of leaving all your doors unlocked.'

Edith, hot and unwholesome-looking in an aertex shirt and a tweed skirt, dropped on to the sofa. From the depths of her shopping basket she produced a wicker handbag embroidered with flowers.

'Now, I want the opinion of someone young and "with it".' Oliver who was forty-two scowled at her, but Nancy, still in her twenties, smiled encouragingly. 'This purse . . .' It was an absurd word, but Edith was too county, too much of a gentlewoman, to talk of handbags unless she meant a small suitcase. 'This purse, will it do for Tamsin's present? It's never been used.' She hesitated in some confusion. 'I mean, of course, it's absolutely new. As a matter of fact I brought it back from Majorca last year. Now, tell me frankly, will it do?'

'Well, she can't very well sling it back at you,' Oliver said rudely. 'Not in front of everyone.' The mention of Majorca reminded him of his second wife's demands. 'Excuse me.' He went outside to get the car.

'I'm sure it'll do beautifully,' Nancy gushed. 'What did Linda say?'

'She said it was square,' Edith said shortly. Her children's failure in achieving the sort of status their parents had wanted for them hurt her bitterly. Linda—Linda who had been at Heathfield—working for Mr. Waller; Roger, coming down from Oxford after a year and going to agricultural

45

college! She would feed them, give them beds in her house, but with other people she preferred to forget their existence.

Nancy said with tactless intuition: 'I thought you weren't terribly keen on the Selbys. Patrick, I mean . . .'

'I've no quarrel with Tamsin. I hope I'm not a vindictive woman.'

'No, but after what Patrick—after him influencing Roger the way he did, I'm surprised you—well, you know what I mean.'

Nancy floundered. The Gavestons weren't really county any more. Their house was no bigger than the Gages'. But still—you'd only got to look at Edith to know her brother lived at Chantflower Grange. I suppose she's only going to the party to have a chance to hob-nob with Crispin Marvell, she thought.

'Patrick Selby behaved very badly, very wrongly,' Edith said. 'And it was just wanton mischief. He's perfectly happy and successful in *his* job.'

'I never quite knew . . .'

'He set out to get at my children. Quite deliberately, my dear. Roger was blissfully happy at The House.' Nancy looked puzzled, thinking vaguely of the Palace of Westminster. 'Christ Church, you know. Patrick Selby got talking to him when he was out with that dog of theirs and the upshot of it was Roger said his father wanted him to go into the business but he wasn't keen. He wanted to be a farmer. As if a boy of nineteen knows what he wants. Patrick said he'd been forced into business when all he wanted was to teach or some absurd thing. He advised Roger to—well, follow his own inclinations. Never mind about us, never mind about poor Paul with no-one to take over the reins at Gavestons, no heir.'

Nancy, greedy for gossip, made sympathetic noises.

'Then, of course, Roger had to say his sister wanted to earn her own living. Made up some stupid tale about our keeping her at home. The next thing was that impossible interfering man suggested she should work in a shop till she was old enough to take up nursing. I don't know why he did it, unless it was because he likes upsetting people. Paul had a great deal to say about it, I assure you. He had quite a stormy interview with Patrick.'

'But it was no good?'

'They do what they like these days.' She sighed and added despondently, 'But as to going tonight, one has one's neighbourhood, one cannot pick and choose these days.'

'Who else is coming?'

'The usual people. The Linchester crowd and Crispin of course. I think it's splendid of him to come so often considering how bitter he must feel.' Edith's sensible, pink-rimmed glasses bobbed on her nose. 'There was a clause in the Marvell contract, you know. No tree felling. Everyone's respected it except Patrick Selby. I know for a fact there were twenty exquisite ancient trees on that plot, and he's had them all down and planted nasty little willows.'

It was just like Oliver, Nancy thought, to come in and spoil it all.

'If you're looking for your cheque book,' she said innocently, 'it's on the record player. While you're about it you might collect my sandals.'

'Oh, are you going to the village?' Edith got up pointedly.

'I'm going into Nottingham.'

'Into *town*? How perfectly splendid. You can give me a lift.'

She picked up the wicker basket and they departed together.

Two fields and a remnant of woodland away Crispin

47

Marvell was sitting in his living room drinking rhubarb wine and writing his history of Chantefleur Abbey. Some days it was easy to concentrate. This was one of the others. He had spent the early part of the morning washing his china and ever since he had replaced the cups in the cabinet and the plates on the walls, he had been unable to keep his eyes from wandering to the glossy surfaces and the warm rich colours. It was almost annoying to reflect what he had been missing in delaying this particular bit of spring-cleaning, the months during which the glaze had been dimmed by winter bloom.

For a moment he mused over the twin olive-coloured plates, one decorated with a life-size apple in relief, the other with a peach; over the Chelsea clock with its tiny dial and opulent figurines of the sultan and his concubine. Marvell kept his correspondence behind this clock and it disturbed him to see the corner of Henry Glide's letter sticking out. He got up and pushed the envelope out of sight between the wall and the Circassian's gold-starred trousers. Then he dipped his pen in the ink-well and returned to Chantefleur.

'The original building had a clerestory of round-headed windows with matching windows in the aisle bays. Only by looking at the Cistercian abbeys now standing in France can we appreciate the effect of the . . .'

He stopped and sighed. Carried away by his own domestic art, he had almost written 'of the glaze on the apple'. It was hardly important. Tomorrow it might rain. He had already spent two years on the history of Chantefleur. Another few months scarcely mattered. In a way, on a wonderful morning like this one, nothing mattered. He gave the plate a last look, running his fingers across the cheek of the apple—the artist had been so faithful he had even pressed in a bruise, there on the underside—and went into the garden.

48

Marvell lived in an almshouse, or rather four almshouses all joined together in a terrace and converted by him into a long low bungalow. The walls were partly of white plaster, partly of rose-coloured brick, and the roof was of pantiles, old now and uneven but made by the hand of a craftsman.

He strolled round the back. Thanks to the bees that lived in three white hives in the orchard the fruit was forming well; they hadn't swarmed this year and he was keeping his fingers crossed. The day spent in carefully cutting out the queen cells had been well worth the sacrifice of half a chapter of Chantefleur. He sat down on the bench. Beyond the hedge in the meadows below Linchester they were cutting the hay. He could hear the baler, that and the sound of the bees. Otherwise all was still.

'All right for some people.'

Marvell turned his head and grinned. Max Greenleaf often came up about this time after his morning calls.

'Come and sit down.'

'It's good to get away from the wasps.' Greenleaf looked at the lichen on the bench, then down at his dark suit. He sat down gingerly.

'There were always a lot of wasps on Linchester,' Marvell said. 'I remember them in the old days. Thousands of damned wasps whenever Mamma gave a garden party.' Greenleaf looked at him suspiciously. An Austrian Jew, he could never escape his conviction that the English landed gentry and the Carinthian aristocracy came out of the same mould. Marvell called it his serfs to the wolves syndrome. 'The wasps are conservative, you see. They haven't got used to the idea that the old house has been gone five years and a lot of company directors' Georgian gone up in its place. They're still on the hunt for Mamma's brandy snaps. Come inside and have a drink.' He smiled at Greenleaf and said in a teasing voice, 'I opened a bottle of mead this morning.'

'I'd rather have a whisky and soda.'

Greenleaf followed him to the house, knocking his head as he always did on the plaque above the front door that said: 1722. Andreas Quercus Fecit. Marvell's reasons for living there were beyond his understanding. The countryside, the flowers, horticulture, agriculture, Marvell's own brand of viticulture, meant nothing to him. He had come to the village to share his brother-in-law's prosperous practice. If you asked him why he lived in Linchester he would answer that it was for the air or that he was obliged to live within a mile or two of his surgery. Modern conveniences, a house that differed inside not at all from a town house, diluted and almost banished those drawbacks. To invite those disadvantages, positively to court them in the form of cesspools, muddy lanes and insectivora as his host did, made Marvell a curio, an object of psychological speculation.

These mysteries of country life reminded him afresh of the cloud on his morning.

'I've just lost a patient,' he said. Marvell, pouring whisky, heard the Austrian accent coming through, a sign that the doctor was disturbed. 'Not my fault, but still . . .'

'What happened?' Marvell drew the curtains, excluding all but a narrow shaft of sunlight that ran across the black oak floor and up Andreas Quercus's squat wall.

'One of the men from Coffley mine. A wasp got on his sandwich and he ate the thing. So what does he do? He goes back to work and the next thing I'm called out because he's choking to death. Asphyxiated before I got there.'

'Could you have done anything?'

'If I'd got there soon enough. The throat closes with the swelling, you see.' Changing the subject, he said: 'You've been writing. How's it coming on?'

'Not so bad. I did my china this morning and it distracted me.' He unhooked the apple plate from the wall and handed it to the doctor. 'Nice?'

Greenleaf took it wonderingly in short thick fingers. 'What's the good of a thing like this? You can't put food on it, can you?' Without aesthetic sense, he probed everything for its use, its material function. This plate was quite useless. Distastefully he imagined eating from it the food he liked best, chopped herring, cucumbers in brine, cabbage salad with caraway seeds. Bits would get wedged under the apple leaves.

'It's purpose is purely decorative,' Marvel laughed. 'Which reminds me, will you be at Tamsin's party?'

'If I don't get called out.'

'She sent me a card. Rather grand. Tamsin always does these things well.' Marvell stretched himself full-length in the armchair. The movement was youthful and the light dim. Greenleaf was seldom deceived about people's ages. He put Marvell's at between forty-seven and fifty-two, but the fine lines which the sun showed up were no longer apparent, and the sprinkling of white hairs was lost in the fair. Probably still attractive to women, he reflected.

'One party after another,' he said, 'Must come expensive.'

'Tamsin has her own income, you know, from her grandmother. She and Patrick are first cousins so she was his grandmother too.'

'But she was the favourite?'

'I don't know about that. He had already inherited his father's business so I daresay old Mrs. Selby thought he didn't need any more.'

'You seem to know a lot about them.'

'I suppose I do. In a way I've been a sort of father confessor to Tamsin. Before they came here they had a flat in

51

Nottingham. Tamsin was lost in the country. When I gave that talk to the Linchester Residents' Association she bombarded me with questions and since then—well, I've become a kind of adopted uncle, Mrs. Beeton and antiquarian rolled into one.'

Greenleaf laughed. Marvell was the only man he knew who could do women's work without becoming old-womanish.

'You know, I don't think she ever really wanted that house. Tamsin loves old houses and old furniture. But Patrick insists on what are called, I believe, uncluttered lines.'

'Tell me, don't you *mind* coming to Linchester?' Always fascinated by other people's emotions, Greenleaf had sometimes wondered about Marvell's reactions to the new houses that had sprung up on his father's estate.

Marvell smiled and shrugged.

'Not really. I'm devoutly thankful I don't have to keep the old place up. Besides it amuses me when I go to parties. I play a sort of mental game trying to fix just where I am in relation to our house.' When Greenleaf looked puzzled he went on, 'What I mean is, when I'm at Tamsin's I always think to myself, the ha-ha came down here and here were the kitchen gardens.' Keeping a straight face he said, 'The Gages' house now, that's where the stables were. I'm not saying it's appropriate, mind.'

'You're scaring me. Makes me wonder about my own place.'

'Oh, you're all right. Father's library and a bit of the big staircase.'

'I don't believe a word of it,' the doctor said and added a little shyly, 'I'm glad you can make a game of the whole thing.'

'You mustn't think,' said Marvell, 'that every time I set foot on Linchester I'm wallowing in a kind of maudlin *recherche du temps perdu.*'

Greenleaf was not entirely convinced. He finished his whisky and remembered belatedly his excuse for the visit.

'And now,' he said, at ease on his own home ground, 'how's the hay fever?'

If the doctor had not perfectly understood Marvell's Proustian reference, he had at least an inkling of its meaning. On Edward Carnaby it would have been utterly lost. His French was still at an elementary stage.

Jo-jo monte. Il est fatigué. Bonne nuit, Jo-jo. Dors bien!

He looked up towards the ceiling and translated the passage into English. Funny stuff for a grown man, wasn't it? All about a kid of five having a bath and going to bed. Still, it was French. At this rate he'd be reading Simenon within the year.

Bonjour, Jo-jo. Quel beau matin! Regarde le ciel. Le soleil brille.

Edward thumbed through the dictionary, looking for *briller.*

'Ted!'

'What is it, dear?' It was funny, but lately he'd got into the habit of calling her dear. She had taken the place of his wife in all ways but one. Sex was lacking but freedom and security took its place. Life was freer with Free, he thought, pleased with his pun.

'If you and Cheryl want your lunch on time you'll have to do something about these wasps, Ted.' She marched in, brisk, neat, womanly, in a cotton frock and frilled apron. He noted with pleasure that she had said lunch and not dinner. Linchester was educating Freda.

'I'll do it right now. Get it over.' He closed the dictionary. *Briller*. To shine, to glow, emit a radiance. The verb perfectly expressed his own mental state. He was glowing with satisfaction and anticipation. *Edouard brille*, he said to himself, chuckling aloud. 'I've promised to pass the stuff on to some people.'

'What people?'

'The gorgeous Mrs. Selby, if you must know. I met her last night and she was all over me. Insisted I go to her party tonight.' Now you couldn't say things like that to a wife. 'She wouldn't take No for an answer,' he said.

Freda sat down.

'You're kidding. You don't know Tamsin.'

'Tamsin! That's all right, that is. Since when have you and her been so pally?'

'And what about me? Where do I come in?'

'Now, look, Free, I'm counting on you to sit in with Cheryl.'

The tears welled into her eyes. After all that had happened, all the love, the promises, the wonderful evenings. Of course it wasn't *his* fault. It was Tamsin's party. But to ask Edward!

'There's no need to get into a tiz. She said I could bring a friend. I don't know about Cheryl, though.'

'Mrs. Staxton'll sit,' Freda said eagerly. 'She's always offering.' Seeing his face still doubtful, his eyes already returning to the French primer, she burst out miserably, 'Ted, I want to go to the party! I've got a right. I've got more right than you.'

Hysteria in Freda was something new. He closed the book.

'What are you talking about?' She was his twin and he could feel the pull of her mind, almost read her thoughts. A terrible unease visited him and he thought of the previous night, the woman's eyes staring past him towards the pond, her sudden unexplained coldness when he had said who he was.

'Freda!'

It all came out then and Edward listened, angry and afraid. The happy mood had gone sour on him.

5

STRINGS of little coloured bulbs festooned the willow trees. As soon as it grew dusk they would be switched on to glow red, orange, green and cold blue against the dark foliage of the oaks in the Millers' garden next door.

Tamsin had shut the food and drink in the dining room away from the wasps. Although she had only seen two throughout the whole day she closed the double windows to be on the safe side. The room was tidy, and apart from the food, bare. Functional, Patrick called it. Now, cleaned by him while Tamsin hovered helplessly in the background, it met even his exacting requirements.

'It is, after all, a *dining* room, not a glory hole,' he had remarked in a chill voice to the vacuum cleaner. To his wife he said nothing, but his look meant Please don't interfere with my arrangements. When the tools were put away and the dusters carefully washed, he had taken the dog to Sherwood Forest, smug, silent with his private joy.

It was too late now to bother with a show of loving obedience. Tamsin dressed, wishing she had something bright and gay, but all her clothes were subdued—to please Patrick. Then she went into the dining room and helped herself to whisky, pouring it straight into a tumbler almost as if it was the last drink she would ever have. Nobody had wished her a happy birthday yet but she had had plenty of cards. Defiantly she took them from the sideboard drawer and arranged them on top of the radiator. There were about a dozen of them, facetious ones showing dishevelled housewives amid piles of crocks; conventional ones (a family of Dartmoor ponies); one whose picture held a secret significance, whose message meant something special to her and to its sender. It was unsigned but Tamsin knew who had sent it. She screwed it up quickly for the sight of it with its cool presumption only deepened her misery.

'Many happy returns of the day, Tamsin,' she said shakily, raising her glass. She sighed and the cards fluttered. Somehow she would have liked to break the glass, hurl it absurdly against Patrick's white wall, because she had come to an end. A new life was beginning. The drink was a symbol of the old life and so was the dress she wore, silver-grey, clinging, expensive. She put the glass down carefully (her old habits died hard), looked at the cards and blinked to stop herself crying. For there should have been one more, bigger than the others, an austere costly card that said To My Wife.

Patrick was never late. He came back on the dot of seven in time to bath and shave and leave the bathroom tidy, and by then she had washed her glass, returning it to its place in the sideboard. She heard the bathroom door close and the key turn in the lock. Patrick was careful about propriety.

Tamsin remained in the dining room for some minutes, feeling an almost suicidal despair. In an hour or so her guests would begin to arrive and they would expect her to be gay because she was young and rich and beautiful and because it was her birthday. If she could get out of the house for a few minutes she might feel better. With Queenie at her heels she took her trug and went down to where the currants grew in what had been the Manor kitchen gardens. The dog lay down in the sun and Tamsin began stripping the bushes of their ripe white fruit.

'I will try to be gay,' she said to herself, or perhaps to the dog, 'for a little while.'

Edward and Freda came up to the front doors of Hallows at a quarter to eight and it was Edward who rang the bell. Freda, whose only reading matter was her weekly women's magazine, had sometimes encountered the cliché 'rooted to the spot' and that was how she felt standing on the swept white stones, immobile, stiff with terror, a sick bile stirring between her stomach and her throat.

No-one came to the door. Freda watched her brother enviously. Not for him the problem of what to do with one's sticky and suddenly over-large hands that twitched and fretted as if seeking some resting place; he had the Vesprid in its brown paper bag to hold.

'Better go round the back,' he said truculently.

It was monastically quiet. The creak of the wrought iron gate made Freda jump as Edward pushed it open. They walked round the side of the house and stopped when they came to the patio. The garden lay before them, waiting, expectant, but not as for a party. It was rather as if it had been prepared for the arrival of some photographer whose carefully angled shots would provide pictures for one of those very magazines. Freda had read a feature the previous week, *Ideal Homesteads in the New Britain,* and the illustrations had shown just such a garden, lawns ribbed in pale and dark green where the mower had crossed them, trees and shrubs whose leaves looked as if they had been individually dusted. At the other end of the patio someone had arranged tables and chairs, some of straw-coloured wicker, others of white-painted twisted metal. A small spark of pleasure and admiration broke across Freda's fear, only to be extinguished almost at once by the sound of water gurgling down a drainpipe behind her ankles. A sign of life, of habitation.

The garden, the house, looked, she thought, as if it hadn't been kept outside at all, as if it had been preserved up to this moment under glass. But she was unable to express this thought in words and instead said foolishly:

'There isn't anybody about. You must have got the wrong night.'

He scowled and she wondered again why he had come, what he was going to say or do. Was it simply kindness to her—for he was, as it were, her key to this house—Tamsin's fascination or something more?

'You won't say anything, will you? You won't say anything to show me up?'

'I told you,' he said. 'I want to see how the land lies, what sort of a mess you've got yourself into. I'm not promising anything, Free.'

Minutes passed, unchanging minutes in which the sleek garden swam before her eyes. Then something happened, something which caused the first crack to appear in Edward's insecure courage.

From behind the willows came a sound familiar to Freda, a long drawn-out bay. Queenie. Edward jerked convulsively and dropped the Vesprid with a clang—a clang like the crack of doom—as the dog bounded from a curtain of shrubs and stopped a yard from him. It was an ominous sound that came from her, a throb rather than an actual noise, and Edward seemed to grow smaller. He picked up the tin and held it in front of him, a ridiculous and wholly inadequate shield.

'Oh, Queenie!' Freda put out her hand. 'It's all right. It's me.'

The dog advanced, wriggling now, to lick the outstretched fingers, when the gate opened and a tall fair man entered the garden. He was wearing a green shirt over slacks and Edward at once felt that his own sports jacket (Harris tweed knocked down to eighty nine and eleven) was unsuitable, an anachronism.

'How do you do?'

He was carrying something that looked like a bottle wrapped in ancient yellowing newspaper, and a huge bunch of roses. The roses were perfect, each bud closed yet about to unfurl, and their stems had been shorn of thorns.

'I don't think we've met. My name's Marvell.'

'Pleased to meet you,' Edward said. He transferred the Vesprid to his left arm and shook hands. 'This is my sister, Miss Carnaby.'

'Where is everyone?'

'We don't know,' Freda said sullenly. 'Till you came we thought we'd got the wrong night.'

'Oh, no, this is Tamsin's birthday.' He pushed Queenie down, smiled suddenly and waved. 'There she is picking my currants, bless her! Will you excuse me?'

'Well!' Freda said. 'If those are county manners you can keep them.'

She watched him stride off down the path and then she saw Patrick's wife. Tamsin got to her feet like a silvery dryad arising from her natural habitat, ran up to Marvell and kissed him on the cheek. They came back together, Tamsin's face buried in roses.

'Josephine Bruce, that's the gorgeous dark red one,' Freda heard her say. 'Virgo, snow-white; Super Star—Oh, lovely, lovely vermilion! And the big peachy beauty—this one—is Peace. You see, Crispin, I *am* learning.'

She stepped on to the greyish-gold stones of the patio and dropped the roses on to a wicker table. The Weimaraner romped over to her and placed her paws on the table's plaited rim.

'And look, lovely mead! You are sweet to me, Crispin.'

'You look like one of those plushy calendars,' Marvell said laughing. 'The respectable kind you see in garages on the Motorway. All girl and dog and flowers and liquor, the good things of life.'

'*Wein, weib und gesang* as Patrick says.' Tamsin's voice was low and her face clouded.

Edward coughed.

'Excuse me,' he said.

'O God, I'm so sorry.' Marvell was crestfallen. 'Tamsin dear, I'm keeping you from your guests.'

Afterwards, looking back, Freda thought Tamsin honestly hadn't known who they were. And after all Edward's stupid airs! Tamsin's face had grown dull and almost ugly; her eyes, large and tawny, seemed to blank out. She stood looking at them still holding a rose against her paintless lips. At last she said:

'I know! The man who goes to evening classes.'

Freda wanted to go then, to slink back against the stone wall, slither between the house and the wattle fence and then run and run until she came to the chalets behind the elms. But Edward was holding her arm. He yanked her forward, exposing her to their gaze like a dealer with his single slave.

'This is my sister. You said I could bring someone.'

Tamsin's face hardened. It was exactly like one of those African art masks, Freda thought, the beautiful goddess one in the saloon bar of that roadhouse on the Southwell road. Freda knew she wasn't going to shake hands.

'Well, now you're here you must have a drink. Masses of drink in the dining room. Where's Patrick?' She looked up to the open windows on the first floor. 'Patrick!'

Edward thrust the Vesprid at her.

'A present? How very sweet of you.'

She pulled the tin out of the bag and giggled. Freda thought she was hysterical—or drunk.

'It's not exactly a present,' Edward said desperately. 'You said to bring it. You said to come early. We could do the wasps.'

'The wasps? Oh, but I've only seen one or two today. We won't worry about wasps.' She flung back the doors and Patrick must have been standing just within. He stepped out poised, smiling, smelling of bath salts. 'Here's my husband. Do go and check the lights, darling.' And she linked her arm into his, smiling brightly.

Freda could feel herself beginning to tremble. She knew her face had paled, then filled with burning blood. Her hand fumbled its way into Patrick's, gaining life and strength as she felt the faint special pressure and the familiar cold touch of his ring. As it came to Edward's turn her heart knocked, but the handshake passed off conventionally. Edward's spirit was broken and he gazed at Patrick dumbly, half-hypnotised.

'What's this?'

Patrick picked up the Vesprid and looked at the label.

Freda couldn't help admiring his aplomb, the coldly masterful way he shook off Tamsin's hand.

'Doesn't it look horrid on my birthday table?' Tamsin bundled the tin back into the paper and pushed it into Edward's arms. She took his fingers in her own and curled them round the parcel. 'There. You look after it, sweetie, or pop it in a safe place. We don't want it mingling with the drinks, do we?'

Then Marvell rescued them and took them into the dining room.

By the time Greenleaf and Bernice got to Hallows everyone had arrived. He had been called out to a man with renal colic and it was eight before he got back. Fortunately Bernice never nagged but waited for him patiently, smoking and playing patience in the morning room.

'I shall wear my alpaca packet,' Greenleaf said. 'So it makes me look like a bowls player? What do I care? I'm not a teenager.'

'No, darling,' said Bernice. 'You're a very handsome mature man. Who wants to be a teenager?'

'Not me, unless you can be one too.'

Well-contented with each other, they set off in a happy frame of mind. They took the short cut across The Green and paused to watch the swans. Greenleaf held his wife's hand.

'At last,' Denholm Smith-King said as they appeared in the patio. 'I was just saying to Joan, is there a doctor in the house?'

'Ha ha,' said Greenleaf mechanically. 'I hope no-one's going to need one. I've come to enjoy myself.' He waved to Tamsin who came from the record-player to greet him. 'Happy birthday. Nice of you to ask us.' He pointed to the now loaded table. 'What's all this?'

'My lovely presents. Look, chocs from Oliver and Nancy, this marvellous bag thing from Edith.' Tamsin held the gifts up in turn, pouting at the bag as she praised it. 'Sweet delicious *marrons glacés* from Joan, and Crispin brought me —what d'you think? Wine and roses. Wasn't that lovely?'

Marvell smiled from behind her, looking boyish. 'Thy shadow, Cynara,' he said. 'The night is thine. . . . '

'So kind! And Bernice . . .' She unwrapped the tiny phial of scent Bernice had put into her hand. 'Nuit de Beltane! How gorgeous. And I've just been telling Nancy how lovely she smells. Imagine, she's wearing it herself. You're all so good to me.' She waved a long brown hand as if their munificence exhausted her, making her more languid than usual.

63

Greenleaf crammed himself into a small wicker armchair. From within the dining room the music had begun the Beguine.

'Your daughter not coming?' he said to Edith Gaveston. She sniffed. 'Much too square for Linda.'

'I suppose so.'

Tamsin had gone, swept away in the arms of Oliver Gage.

'If you've a minute,' said Denholm Smith-King,' I've been meaning to ask you for ages. It's about a lump I've got under my arm. . . .'

Greenleaf, preparing for a busman's holiday, took the drink Patrick held out to him, but Smith-King was temporarily diverted. He looked quickly about him as if to make sure that most of the others were dancing, and he touched Patrick's arm nervously.

'Oh, Pat old man. . . .'

'Not now, Denholm.' Patrick's smile was brief, mechanical, gone in a flash. 'I don't care to mix business with pleasure.'

'Later, then?'

Patrick glanced at the ashtray Smith-King was filling with stubs, opened the cigarette box insolently and let the lid fall almost instantly.

'I'm not surprised you've got a lump,' he said, 'but don't bore my guests, will you?'

'Funny chap,' Smith-King said and an uneasy flush seeped across his face. 'Doesn't care what he says.' The red faded as Patrick strolled away. 'Now about this said lump. . . .'

Greenleaf turned towards him and tried to look as if he was listening while keeping his thoughts and half an eye on the other guests.

Most of them were his patients except the Selbys and the Gavestons who were on Dr. Howard's private list, but he sized them up now from a psychological rather than a medical standpoint. As he sometimes said to Bernice, he had to know about human nature, it was part of his job.

The Carnabys now, they weren't enjoying themselves. They sat apart from the rest in a couple of deck chairs on the lawn and they weren't talking to each other. Freda had hidden her empty shandy glass under the seat; Carnaby, like a parent clutching his rejected child, sat dourly, holding what looked like a tin in one of Waller's paper wrappings.

Beyond them among the currant bushes Marvell was showing Joan and Nancy the ancient glories of the Manor kitchen gardens. Greenleaf knew little about women's fashions but Nancy's dress looked out of place to him, ill-fitting (she'll have to watch her weight, said the medical part of him, or her blood pressure will go soaring up in ten years' time). It contrasted badly with the expensive scent she wore, whiffs of which he had caught while they were standing together by Tamsin's birthday table. Why, incidentally, had Gage looked black as thunder when Bernice handed over their own phial of perfume?

He was dancing with Tamsin now and of the three couples on the floor they were the best matched. Clare and Walter Miller lumbered past him, resolutely fox-trotting out of time. Rather against her will Bernice had been coaxed into the stiff arms of old Paul Gaveston who, too conscious of the proprieties to hold her close, stared poker-faced over her shoulder, his embracing hand a good two inches from her back. Greenleaf smiled to himself. Gage was without such inhibitions. His smooth dusky cheek was pressed close to Tamsin's, his body fused with hers. They hardly moved but swayed slowly, almost indecently, on a square yard of floor. Well, well, thought Greenleaf. The music died away and broke suddenly into a mambo.

'The thing is,' Smith-King was saying, 'it's getting bigger. No getting away from it.'

'I'd better take a look at it,' Greenleaf said.

A fourth couple had joined the dancers. Greenleaf felt relieved. Patrick was a difficult fellow at the best of times but he could rise to an occasion. It was nice to see him rescuing the Carnaby girl and dancing with her as if he really wanted to.

'You will?' Smith-King half-rose. His movement seemed to sketch the shedding of garments.

'Not now,' Greenleaf said, alarmed. 'Come down to the surgery.'

The sun had quite gone now, even the last lingering rays, and dusk was coming to the garden. Tamsin had broken away from Gage and gone to switch on the fairy lights. But for the intervention of his wife who marched on to the patio exclaiming loudly about the gnats, Gage would have followed her.

'How I hate beastly insects,' Nancy grumbled. 'You'd think with all this D.D.T. and everything there just wouldn't be any more mosquitos.' She glared at Marvell. 'I feel itchy all over.'

As if at a signal Walter Miller and Edith Gaveston broke simultaneously into gnat-bite anecdotes. Joan Smith-King gravitated towards Greenleaf as people so often did with minor ailments even on social occasions, and stood in front of him scratching her arms. He got up at once to let her sit next to her husband but as he turned he saw that Denholm's chair was empty. Then he saw him standing in the now deserted dining room confronting Patrick. The indispensable cigarette was in his mouth. Greenleaf couldn't hear what he was saying, only Joan's heavy breathing loud and strained above the buzz of conversation. The cigarette trembled, adhering to Denholm's lip, and his hands moved in a gesture of hopelessness. Patrick laughed suddenly and turning away, strode into the garden as the lights came on.

Greenleaf, not sensitive to a so-called romantic atmosphere, was unmoved by the strings of coloured globes. But most of the women cried out automatically. Fairy lights were the thing; they indicated affluence, taste, organisation. With little yelps of delight Nancy ran up and down, pointing and exhorting the others to come and have a closer look.

'So glad you like them,' Tamsin said. 'We do.' Patrick coughed, dissociating himself. He was taking his duties to heart, Greenleaf thought, watching his hand enclose Freda Carnaby's in a tight grip.

'Now, have we all got drinks?' Tamsin reached for Marvell's empty glass. 'Crispin, your poor arms!'

'There are mosquitos at the bottom of your garden,' Marvell said, laughing. 'I meant to bring some citronella but I forgot.'

'Oh, but we've got some. I'll get it.'

'No, I'll go. You want to dance.'

Gage had already claimed her, his arm about her waist.

'I'll tell you where it is. It's in the spare bedroom bathroom. Top shelf of the cabinet.'

Joan Smith-King was giggling enviously.

'Oh, do you have two bathrooms? How grand!'

'Just through the spare room,' Tamsin said, ignoring her, 'You know the way.'

The expression in her eyes shocked Greenleaf. It was as if, he thought, she was playing some dangerous game.

'I'm being absurd,' he said to Bernice.

'Oh, no, darling, you're such a practical man. Why are you being absurd anyway?'

'Nothing,' Greenleaf said.

Marvell came back holding a bottle. He had already unstoppered it and was anointing his arms.

'Thank you so much,' he said to Tamsin, 'Madame Tussaud.'

Tamsin gabbled at him quickly.

'You found the stuff? Marvellous. No, sweetie, that isn't a pun. Come and dance.'

'I am for other than for dancing measures,' Marvell laughed. 'I've been in the chamber of horrors and I need a drink.' He helped himself from the sideboard. 'You might have warned me.'

'What *do* you mean, chamber of horrors?' Nancy was wide-eyed. The party was beginning to flag and she was eager for something to buoy it up and, if possible, prise Oliver away from Tamsin. 'Have you been seeing ghosts?'

'Something like that.'

'Tell, tell!'

Suddenly Tamsin whirled away from Oliver and throwing up her arms, seized Marvell to spin him away past the record player, past the birthday table, across the patio and out on to the lawn.

'Let's all go,' she cried. 'Come and see the skeleton in the cupboard!'

They began to file out into the hall, the women giggling expectantly. Marvell went first, his drink in his hand. Only Patrick hung back until Freda took his hand and whispered something to him. Even Smith-King, usually obtuse, noticed his unease.

'Lead on, Macduff!' he said.

6

I F I T had been earlier in the day or even if the lights had been on it would have looked very different. But as it was—day melting into night, the light half-gone and the air so still that nothing moved, not even the net curtains at the open windows—the effect was instant and, for a single foolish moment, shocking.

Marvell pulled a face. The other men stared, Paul Gaveston making a noise that sounded like a snort. Smith-King whistled, then broke into a hearty laugh.

The women expressed varying kinds of horror, squeals, hands clamped to mouths, but only Freda sounded genuinely distressed. She was standing close to Greenleaf. He heard her low gasp and felt her shudder.

'Definitely not my cup of tea,' Nancy said. 'Imagine forgetting it was there and then coming face to face with it in the night on your way to the loo!'

Greenleaf was suddenly sickened. Of all the people in the Selbys' spare room he was the only one who had ever seen an actual head that had been severed from an actual body. The first one he had encountered as a student, the second had been the subject of a post-mortem conducted on a man decapitated in a railway accident. Because of this and for other reasons connected with his psychological make-up, he was at the same time more and less affected by the picture than were the other guests.

It was a large picture, an oil painting in a frame of scratched gilt, and it stood propped on the floor against the watered silk wallpaper. Greenleaf knew nothing at all about painting and the view many people take that all life—or all death—is a fit subject for art would have appalled him. Of brushwork, of colour, he was ignorant, but he knew a good deal about anatomy and a fair amount about sexual perversion. Therefore he was able to admire the artist for his accuracy—the hewn neck on the silver platter showed the correct vertebra and the jugular in its proper place—and deplore a mentality which thought sadism a suitable subject for entertainment. Greenleaf hated cruelty; all the suffering of all his ancestors in the ghettos of Eastern Europe was strong within him. He stuck out his thick underlip, took off his glasses and began polishing them on his alpaca jacket.

Thus he was unable to see for a moment the face of the man who stood near him on the other side of Freda Carnaby, the man whose house this was. But he heard the intake of breath and the faint smothered cry.

'But just look at the awful way she's staring at that ghastly head,' Nancy cried, clutching Oliver's hand. 'I think I ought to understand what it means, but I don't.'

'Perhaps it's just as well,' her husband said crisply.

'What is it, Tamsin? What's it supposed to be?'

Tamsin had drawn her finger across the thick painted surface, letting a nail rest at the pool of blood.

'Salome and John the Baptist,' Marvell said. He was quickly bored by displays of naiveté and he had gone to the window. Now he turned round, smiling. 'Of course she wouldn't have been dressed like that. The artist put her in contemporary clothes. Who painted it, Tamsin?'

'I just wouldn't know,' Tamsin shrugged. 'It was my grandmother's. I lived with her, you see, and I grew up with it, so it doesn't affect me all that much any more. I used to love it when I was a little girl. Too dreadful of me! '

'You're never going to hang it on the wall?' Clare Miller asked.

'I might. I don't know yet. When my grandmother died two years ago she left all her furniture to a friend, a Mrs. Prynne. I happened to be visiting her a couple of months ago and of course I absolutely drooled over this thing. So she said she's send it to me for my birthday and here it is.'

'Rather you than I.'

Tamsin giggled.

'I might put it on the dining-room wall. D'you think it would go well with a grilled steak?'

They had all looked at the picture. Everyone had said something if only to exclaim with thrilled horror. Only Patrick had kept silent and Greenleaf, puzzled, turned now to look at him. Patrick's face was deathly white under the cloud of freckles. Somehow the freckles made him look worse, the pallor of his skin blotched with what looked like bruises. When at last he spoke his voice was loud and un-steady and the icy poise quite gone.

'All right,' he said, 'the joke's over. Excuse me.' He pushed at Edward Carnaby, shoving him aside with his shoulder and stripping the counterpane from one of the beds, flung it across the picture. But instead of catching on the topmost beading of the frame it slipped and fell to the floor. The effect of its falling, like the sweeping away of a curtain, exposed the picture with a sudden vividness. The gloating eyes, the parted lips and the plump bosom of Herod's niece arose before them in the gloom. She seemed to be watching with a dreadful satisfaction the slithering silk as it unveiled the trophy in the dish.

'You bitch! ' Patrick said.

There was a shocked silence. Then Tamsin stepped forward and looped the counterpane up. Salome was veiled.

'Oh, really!' she said. 'It was just a joke, darling. You *are* rude.'

Smith-King moved uneasily.

'Getting late, Joanie,' he said. 'Beddy-byes.'

'It's not ten yet.' Tamsin caught Patrick's hand and leaning towards him, kissed him lightly on the cheek. He remained quite still, the colour returning to his face, but he didn't look at her. 'We haven't eaten yet. All that lovely food!'

'Ah, food.' Smith-King rubbed his hands together. It would be another story if a scene could be avoided and Patrick perhaps yet made amenable. 'Must keep body and soul together.'

'The wolf from the door?' Marvell said softly.

'That's the ticket.' He slapped Marvell on the back.

Patrick seemed to realise that his hand was still resting in Tamsin's. He snatched it away, marched out of the room and down the stairs, his dignity returning. With a defiant glance at Tamsin, Freda followed him.

'It's a lovely night,' Tamsin cried. 'Let's go into the garden and take the food with us.' Her eyes were very bright. She linked her arm into Oliver's and as an afterthought clasped Nancy's hand and swung it. 'Eat, drink and be merry for tomorrow we die!'

They went downstairs and Tamsin danced into the dining-room. Greenleaf thought they had seen the last of Patrick for that night, but he was on the patio, subdued, his face expressionless, arranging plates on the wicker tables. Freda Carnaby stood by him, sycophantic, adoring.

'Well!' said Nancy Gage. She pulled her chair up alongside Greenleaf's. 'I thought Patrick made an exhibition of

72

himself, didn't you? Immature I call it, making all that fuss about a picture.'

'It is the eye of childhood that fears a painted devil.' Marvell passed her a plate of smoked salmon rolled up in brown bread.

'Juvenile,' Nancy said. 'I mean, it's not as if it was a film. I don't mind admitting I've seen some horror films that have absolutely terrified me. I've wakened in the night bathed in perspiration, haven't I, Oliver?' Oliver was too far away to hear. He sat on the stone wall in gloomy conference with Tamsin.

Nancy, beckoning to him, raised the salmon roll blindly to her mouth.

'Look out!' Greenleaf said quickly. He knocked the roll out of her hand. 'A wasp,' he explained as she jumped. 'You were going to eat it.'

'Oh, no!' Nancy leapt to her feet and shook her skirt. 'I hate them. I'm terrified of them.'

'It's all right. It's gone.'

'No, it hasn't. Look, there's another one.' Nancy flapped her arms as a wasp winged past her face, circled her head and alighted on a fruit flan. 'Oliver, there's one in my hair!'

'What on earth's the matter?' Tamsin got up reluctantly and came between the tables. 'Oh, wasps. Too maddening.' She was taller than Nancy and she blew lightly on to the fair curls. 'It's gone, anyway.'

'You shouldn't have brought the food out,' Patrick said. 'You would do it.' Since he had been the first to do so, this Greenleaf thought, was hardly fair. 'I hate this damned inefficiency. Look, dozens of them!'

Everyone had pushed back their chairs, leaving their food half-eaten. The striped insects descended upon the tables making first for fruit and cream. They seemed to drop from the skies and they came quite slowly, wheeling first above the

73

food with a sluggish yet purposeful concentration like enemy aircraft engaged in a reconnaissance. Then, one by one, they dropped upon pastry and jelly, greedy for the sweet things. Their wings vibrated.

'Well, that's that,' Tamsin said. Her hand dived for a plate of petit fours but she withdrew it quickly with a little scream. 'Get off me, hateful wasp! Patrick, do something.' He was standing beside her but farther removed perhaps than he had ever been. Exasperated and bored, his hands in his pockets, he stared at the feasting insects. 'Get the food in!'

'It's a bit late for that,' Marvell said. 'They're all over the dining-room.' He looked roofwards. 'You've got a nest, you know.'

'That doesn't surprise me at all,' said Walter Miller who lived next door. 'I said to Clare only yesterday, you mark my words, I said, the Selbys have got a wasp nest in their roof.'

'What are we going to do about it?'

'Kill them.' Edward Carnaby had opened his mouth to no one except his sister since, on their arrival, Tamsin had snubbed him. Now his hour had come. 'Exterminate them,' he said. He pulled the tin of Vesprid from its bag and dumped it in the middle of the table where Nancy, Marvell and Greenleaf had been sitting. 'You should have let me do it before,' he said to Tamsin.

'Do it? Do what?' Tamsin looked at the Vesprid. 'What do you do, spray it on them?'

Edward seemed to be about to embark on a long technical explanation. He took a deep breath.

Walter Miller said quickly: 'You'll want a ladder. There's one in my garage.'

'Right,' said Edward. 'The first thing is to locate the nest. I'll need someone to give me a hand.' Marvell got up.

'No, Crispin, Patrick will go.' Tamsin touched her husband's arm. 'Come on, darling. You can't let your guests do all the work.'

For a moment he looked as if he could. He glanced mulishly from Marvell to his wife. Then, without speaking to or even looking at Edward, he started to walk towards the gate.

'Blood sports, Tamsin,' Marvell said. 'Your parties are unique.'

When Patrick and Edward came back carrying Miller's ladder the others had moved out on to the lawn. By now the patio was clouded with wasps. Droves of them gathered on the tables. The less fortunate late-comers zoomed enviously a yard above their fellows, fire-flies in the radiance from the fairy lights.

Edward propped the ladder against the house wall. Making sure his heroics were witnessed, he thrust a hand among the cakes and grabbed one swiftly. Then he unscrewed the cap on the Vesprid tin and poured a little liquid on to the pastry.

'You'd better nip up to the spare bedroom,' he said to Patrick importantly. 'I reckon the nest's just above the bathroom window.'

'What for?' Patrick had paled and Greenleaf thought he knew why.

'I shall want some more light, shan't I?' Edward was enjoying himself. 'And someone'll have to hand this to me.' He made as if to thrust the poisoned cake into his host's hand.

'*I* am going up the ladder,' Patrick said icily.

Edward began to argue. He was the expert, wasn't he? Hadn't he just dealt efficiently with a nest of his own?

'Oh, for heaven's sake!' Tamsin said. 'This is supposed to be my birthday party.'

In the end Edward went rebelliously indoors carrying his bait. Marvell stood at the bottom of the ladder, steadying it, and when a light appeared at the bathroom window, Patrick began to climb. From the lawn they watched him peer along the eaves, his face white and tense in the patch of light. Then he called out with the only flash of humour he had permitted himself that evening:

'I've found it. Apparently there's no-one at home.'

'I reckon they've all gone to a party,' Edward called. Delighted because someone on the lawn had laughed, he licked his lips and pushed the cake towards Patrick. 'Supper,' he said.

Greenleaf found himself standing close by Oliver Gage and he turned to him to make some comment on the proceedings, but something in the other man's expression stopped him. He was staring at the figure on the ladder and his narrow red lips were wet. Greenleaf saw that he was clenching and unclenching his hands.

'Oh, look! What's happening?' Suddenly Nancy clutched Greenleaf's arm and startled he looked roofwards.

Patrick had started violently, arching his back away from the ladder. He shouted something. Then they saw him wince, hunch his shoulders and cover his face with his free arm.

'He's been stung,' Greenleaf heard Gage say flatly, 'and serve him bloody well right.' He didn't move but Greenleaf hurried forward to join the others who had gathered at the foot of the ladder. Three wasps were encircling Patrick's head, wheeling about him and making apparently for his closed eyes. They saw him for a moment, fighting, both arms flailing, his blind face twisted. Then Edward disappeared and the light went out. Now Patrick was just a silhouette against the clear turquoise sky and to Greenleaf he looked like a marionette of crumpled black paper whose convulsively beating arms seemed jerked by unseen strings.

'Come down!' Marvell shouted.

'O God!' Patrick gave a sort of groan and collapsed against the rungs, swaying precariously.

Someone shouted: 'He's going to fall,' but Patrick didn't fall. He began to slide down, prone against the ladder, and his shoes caught on each rung as he descended, tap, tap, flap, until he fell into Marvell's arms.

'Are you all right?' Marvell and Greenleaf asked together and Marvell shied at the wasp that came spiralling down towards Patrick's head. 'They've gone. Are you all right?'

Patrick said nothing but shuddered and put up his hand to cover his cheek. Behind him Greenleaf heard Freda Carnaby whimpering like a puppy, but nobody else made a sound. In the rainbow glimmer they stood silent and peering like a crowd at a bullfight who have seen a hated matador come to grief. The hostility was almost tangible and there was no sound but the steady buzz of the wasps.

'Come along.' Greenleaf heard his own voice pealing like a bell. 'Let's get him into the house.' But Patrick shook off his arm and blundered into the dining room.

They gathered round him in the lounge, all except Marvell who had gone to the kitchen to make coffee. Patrick crouched in an armchair holding his handkerchief against his face. He had been stung in several places, under the left eye, on the left wrist and forearm and on the right arm in what Greenleaf called the cubital fossa.

'Lucky it wasn't a good deal worse,' Edward said peevishly.

Patrick's eye was already beginning to swell and close. He scowled at Edward and said rudely:

'Get lost!'

'Please don't quarrel.' No-one knew how Freda had insinuated herself into her position on the footstool at Patrick's knees, nor exactly when she had taken his hand. 'It's bad enough as it is.'

'Oh, really,' Tamsin said. 'Such a fuss! Excuse me, will you? It might be a good idea for my husband to get some air.'

For the second time that night Denholm Smith-King looked first at his watch, then at his wife. 'Well, we'll be getting along. You won't want us.'

Marvell had come in with the coffee things but Tamsin didn't argue. She lifted her cheek impatiently for Joan to kiss.

'Coffee, Nancy? Oliver?' She by-passed the Carnabys exactly as if they were pieces of furniture. Oliver rejected the cup coldly, sitting on the edge of his chair.

'Perhaps we'd better go too.' Nancy looked hopelessly from angry face to angry face. 'Have you got any bi-carb? It's wonderful for wasp stings. I remember when my sister . . .'

'Come *along*, Nancy,' Oliver said. He took Nancy's arm and pulled her roughly. It looked as if he was going to leave without another word, but he stopped at the door and took Tamsin's hand. Their eyes met, Tamsin's wary, his, unless Greenleaf was imagining things, full of pleading disappointment. Then when Nancy kissed her, he followed suit, touching her cheek with the sexless peck that was common politeness on Linchester.

When they had gone, taking the Gavestons with them, and the Willises and the Millers had departed by the garden gate, Greenleaf went over to Patrick. He examined his eye and asked him how he felt.

'Lousy.'

Greenleaf poured him a cup of coffee.

'Had I better send for Dr. Howard, Max?' Tamsin didn't

look anxious or excited or uneasy any more. She just looked annoyed.

'I don't think so.' Howard, he knew for a fact, wasn't on the week-end rota. A substitute would come and—who could tell?—that substitute might be himself. 'There's not much you can do. Perhaps an anti-histamine. I'll go over home and fetch something.'

Bernice and Marvell went with him, but he came back alone. The Carnabys were still there. Tamsin had left the front doors open for him and as he crossed the hall he heard no voices. They were all sitting in silence, each apparently nursing private resentment. Freda had moved a little way away from Patrick and had helped herself to coffee.

As if taking her cue from his arrival, Tamsin said sharply: 'Isn't it time you went?' She spoke to Edward but she was looking at Freda. 'When you've quite finished, of course.'

'I'm sure I didn't mean to be *de trop.*' Edward blushed but he brought out his painfully acquired French defiantly. Freda lingered woodenly. Then Patrick gave her a little push, a sharp sadistic push that left a red mark on her arm.

'Run along, there's a good girl,' he said and she rose obediently, pulling her skirt down over her knees.

' 'Night,' Patrick said abruptly. He pushed past Edward, ignoring the muttered 'We know when we're not wanted.' At the door he said to Greenleaf, 'You'll come up?' and the doctor nodded.

When he entered the balcony room behind Tamsin, Patrick was already in bed and he lay with his arms outside the sheets, the stings covered by blue pyjama sleeves.

By now his face was almost unrecognisable. The cheek had swollen and closed the eye. He looked, Greenleaf thought, rather as if he had mumps.

Queenie was stretched beside him, her feet at the foot of the bed, her jowls within the palm of his hand.

'You'll be too hot with him there,' the doctor said.

'It's not a him, it's a bitch.' Tamsin put her hand on Queenie's collar and for a moment Patrick's good eye blazed. 'Oh, all right, but I shan't sleep. I feel like hell.'

Greenleaf opened the windows to the balcony. The air felt cool, almost insolently fresh and invigorating after the hot evening. There were no curtains here to sway and alarm a sleeper, only the white hygienic blinds.

'Do you want something to make you sleep?' Prudently Greenleaf had brought his bag back with him. But Tamsin moved over to the dressing-table with its long built-in counter of black glass and creamy wood textured like watered silk. She opened one of the drawers and felt inside.

'He's got these,' she said. 'He had bad insomnia last year and Dr. Howard gave them to him.'

Greenleaf took the bottle from her. Inside were six blue capsules. Sodium Amytal, two hundred milligrammes.

'He can have one.' He unscrewed the cap and rattled a capsule into the palm of his hand.

'One's no good,' Patrick said. He held his cheek to lessen the pain talking caused him, and Tamsin, white and fluttering against her own reflection in the black glass wardrobe doors, nodded earnestly. 'He always had to have two,' she said.

'One.' Greenleaf was taking no chances. He opened his bag and took out a phial. 'The anti-histamine will help you to sleep. You'll sleep like a log.'

Patrick took them all at once, drinking from the glass Tamsin held out to him. 'Thanks,' he said. Tamsin waited until the doctor had fastened his bag and replaced the capsules in the immaculately tidy drawer. Then she switched off the light and they went downstairs.

80

'Please don't say Thank you for a lovely party,' she said when she and Greenleaf were in the hall.

Greenleaf chuckled. 'I won't,' he said.

The swans had gone to bed long ago in the reeds on the edge of the pond. From the woods between Linchester and Marvell's house something cried out, a fox perhaps or just an owl. It could have been either for all Greenleaf knew. His short stocky body cast a long shadow in the moonlight as he crossed The Green to the house called Shalom. He was suddenly very tired.

Marvell, on the other hand, was wide awake. He walked home through the woods slowly, reaching out from time to time to touch the moist lichened tree trunks in the dark. There were sounds in the forest, strange crunching whispering sounds which would have alarmed the doctor. Marvell had known them since boyhood, the tread of the fox—this was only a few miles north of Quorn country—the soft movement of dry leaves as a grass snake shifted them. It was very dark but the darkness was not absolute. Each trunk was a grey signpost to him; leaves touched his face and although the air was sultry they were cold and clean against his cheek. As he came out into Long Lane he heard in the distance the cry of the nightjar and he sighed.

When he had let himself into the house he lit one of the oil lamps and went as he always did before going to bed from room to room to look at his treasures. The porcelain gleamed, catching up what little light there was. He held the lamp for a moment against the mezzotint of Rievaulx. It recalled to him his own work on another Cistercian abbey and, setting the lamp by the window, he sat down with his manuscript, not to write—it was too late for that—but to read what he had written that day.

Red and white by the window. The snowflake fronds of the

Russian Vine and beside it hanging like drops of crimson wax, Berberidopsis, blood-red, absurdly named. The moonlight and the lamplight met and something seemed to pierce his heart.

Moths seeing the light, came at once to the lattice and a coal-black one — Marvell recognised it as The Chimney Sweeper's Boy—fluttered in at the open casement. It was followed by a larger, greyish-white one, its wings hung with filaments, swansdown in miniature. For a second Marvell watched them seek the lamp. Then, fearful lest they burn their wings, he gathered them up, making a loose cage of his hands, and thrust them out of the window.

They spiralled away from yellow into silvery light. He looked and looked again. There was someone in the garden. A shape, itself moth-like, was moving in the orchard. He brushed the black and white wing dust from his hands and leaned out to see who was paying him a visit at midnight.

7

ON Sunday morning Greenleaf got up at eight, did some exercises which he told his patients confidently would reduce their waist measurements from thirty-four to twenty-nine, and had a bath. By nine he had looked at *The Observer* and taken a cup of coffee up to Bernice. Then he sat down to write to his two sons who were away at school.

It was unlikely that anyone would call him out today. He had done his Sunday stint on the Chantflower doctors' rota, the previous week-end, and he intended to have a lazy day. Bernice appeared at about ten and they had a leisurely breakfast, talking about the boys and about the new car which ought to arrive in time to fetch them home for the holidays. After a while they took their coffee into the garden. They were near enough to the house to hear the phone but when it rang Greenleaf let Bernice answer it, knowing it wouldn't be for him.

But instead of settling down to a good gossip Bernice came back quickly, looking puzzled. This was odd, for Bernice seldom hurried.

'It's Tamsin, darling,' she said. 'She wants you.'

'Me?'

'She's in a state, but she wouldn't tell me anything. All she said was I want Max.'

Greenleaf took the call on the morning room phone.

'Max? It's Tamsin.' For almost the first time since he had

met her Tamsin wasn't using her affected drawl. 'I know I shouldn't be ringing you about this but I can't get hold of Dr. Howard.' She paused and he heard her inhale as if on a cigarette. 'Max, I can't wake Patrick. He's awfully cold and I've shaken him but . . . he doesn't wake.'

'When was this?'

'Just now, this minute. I overslept and I've only just got up.'

'I'll be right over,' Greenleaf said.

She murmured, 'Too kind!' and he heard the receiver drop.

Taking up his bag, he went by the short cut, the diameter of The Circle across the grass. On the face of it it seemed obvious what had happened. In pain from his stings Patrick had taken an extra one of the capsules. I ought to have taken the damned things away with me, Greenleaf said to himself. But still, it wasn't for him to baby another man's patients. Howard had prescribed them, they were safe enough unless . . . Unless! Surely Patrick wouldn't have been fool enough to take *two* more? Greenleaf quickened his pace and broke into a trot. Patrick was a young man, apparently healthy, but still, three . . . And the anti-histamine. Suppose he had taken the whole bottleful?

She was waiting for him on the doorstep when he ran up the Hallows drive and she hadn't bothered to dress. Because she never made up her face and always wore her hair straight she hadn't the bleak unkempt look of most of the women who called him out in an emergency. She wore a simple expensive dressing-gown of candy-striped cotton, pink and white with a small spotless white bow at the neck, and there were silver chain sandals on her feet. She looked alarmed and because of her fear, very young.

'Oh, Max, I didn't know what to do.'

'Still asleep, is he?'

Greenleaf went upstairs quickly, talking to her over his shoulder.

'He's so white and still and—and heavy somehow.'

'All right. Don't come up. Make some coffee. Make it very strong and black.'

She went away to the kitchen and Greenleaf entered the bedroom. Patrick was lying on his back, his head at an odd angle. His face was still puffy and the arms which were stretched over the counterpane, faintly swollen and white, not red any more. Greenleaf knew that colour, the yellowish ivory of parchment, and that waxen texture.

He took one of the wrists and remembered what Tamsin had said about the heavy feeling. Then, having slipped one hand within the bedclothes, he lifted Patrick's eyelids and closed them again. He sighed deeply. Feeling Patrick's pulse and heart had been just a farce. He had known when he came into the room. The dead look so very dead, as if they have never been alive.

He went out to meet Tamsin. She was coming up the stairs with the dog behind her.

'Tamsin, come in here.' He opened the door to the room where last night they had looked at the picture. One of the beds had been slept in and the covers were thrown back. 'Would you like to sit down?'

'Can't you wake him either?'

'I'm afraid . . .' He was a friend and he put his arm about her shoulders. 'You must be prepared for a shock.' She looked up at him. He had never noticed how large her eyes were nor of what a curious shade of transparent amber. 'I'm very much afraid Patrick is dead.'

She neither cried nor cried out. There was no change of colour in the smooth brown skin. Resting back against the bed-head, she remained as still as if she too were dead. She seemed to be thinking. It was as if, Greenleaf thought, all her past life with Patrick was being re-lived momentarily within her brain. At last she shuddered and bowed her head.

'What was it?' He had to bend towards her to catch the words. 'The cause, I mean. What did he die of?'

'I don't know.'

'The wasp stings?'

Greenleaf shook his head.

'I don't want to trouble you now,' he said gently, 'but those capsules, the sodium amytal, where are they?'

Tamsin got up like a woman in a dream.

'In the drawer. I'll get them.'

He followed her back into the other bedroom. She looked at Patrick, still without crying, and Greenleaf expected her to kiss the pallid forehead. They usually did. When instead she turned away and went to the dressing table he drew the sheet up over Patrick's face.

'There are still five in the bottle,' she said, and held it out to him. Greenleaf was very surprised. He felt a creeping unease.

'I'll get on to Dr. Howard,' he said.

Howard was out playing golf. Mrs. Howard would ring the club and her husband would come straight over. When Greenleaf walked into the dining room Tamsin was kneeling on the floor with her arms round the neck of the Weimaraner. She was crying.

'Oh, Queenie! Oh, Queenie!'

The room was untouched since the night before. The drinks were still on the sideboard and out on the patio some of the food still remained: heat-curled bread, melting cream, a shrivelled sandwich on a doyley. On the birthday table Marvell's roses lay among the other gifts, pearled with Sunday's dew. Greenleaf poured some brandy into a glass and handed it to Tamsin.

'How long has he been dead?' she asked.

'A good while,' Greenleaf said. 'Hours. Perhaps ten or twelve hours. Of course you looked in on him before you went to bed?'

She had stopped crying. 'Oh, yes,' she said.

'It doesn't matter. I don't want to upset you.'

'That's all right, Max. I'd like to talk about it.'

'You didn't sleep in the same room?'

'Not when one of us was ill,' Tamsin said quickly. 'I thought if he was restless it would be better for me to go in the back. Restless!' She passed her hand across her brow. 'Too dreadful, Max!' She went on rather as if she were giving evidence, using clipped sentences. 'I tried to clear up the mess in the garden but I was too tired. Then I looked in on Patrick. It must have been about midnight. He was sleeping then. I know he was, he was breathing. Well, then I went to bed. I was terribly tired, Max, and I didn't wake up till eleven. I rushed into Patrick because I couldn't hear a sound. Queenie had come up on my bed during the night.' Her hand fumbled for the dog's neck and she pushed her fingers into the plushy fur. 'I couldn't wake him so I phoned Dr. Howard. You know the rest.'

Patrick had died, Greenleaf thought, as he had lived, precisely, tidily, without dirt or disorder. Not for him the sloppy squalor that attended so many death-beds. From mild discomfort he had slipped into sleep, from sleep into death.

'Tamsin,' he said slowly and kindly, 'have you got any other sleeping pills in the house? Have you got any of your own?'

'Oh, no. No, I know we haven't. Patrick just had those six left and I never need anything to make me sleep.' She added unnecessarily: 'I sleep like a log.'

'Had he a weak heart? Did you ever hear of any heart trouble?'

'I don't think so. We'd been married for seven years, you

87

know, but I've known Patrick since he was a little boy. I don't know if you knew we were cousins? His father and mine were brothers.'

'No serious illnesses?'

A petulant cloud crossed her face briefly. 'He was born in Germany,' she said. 'Then, when the war came, they lived in America. After they came back to this country they used to come and see us sometimes. Patrick was terribly spoiled, coddled really. They used to make him wrap up warm even in the summer and I had swimming lessons but they wouldn't let him. I always thought it was because they'd lived in California.' She paused, frowning. 'He was always all right when he was grown-up. The only time he went to Dr. Howard was when he couldn't sleep.'

'I think you will have to prepare yourself,' Greenleaf said, 'for the possibility of an inquest, or, at any rate, a post-mortem.'

She nodded earnestly.

'Oh, quite,' she said. 'I understand. That'll be absolutely all right.' She might have been agreeing to cancel an engagement, so matter-of-fact was her tone.

After that they sat in silence, waiting for Dr. Howard to come. The Weimaraner went upstairs and they heard her claws scraping, scraping at the closed door of the balcony room.

As things turned out, it never came to an inquest. Greenleaf stood in at the post-mortem because he was interested and because the Selbys had been friends of his. Patrick had died, like all the dead, of heart failure. The death certificate was signed and he was buried in Chantflower cemetery on the following Thursday.

Greenleaf and Bernice went to the funeral. They took Marvell with them in Bernice's car.

'Blessed are the dead,' said the Rector, a shade sardonically, 'which die in the Lord.' Since coming to Linchester Patrick had never been to church.

Patrick's parents were dead; Tamsin had been an orphan since she was four. They had both been only children. Consequently there were no relatives at the graveside. Apart from the Linchesterites, only three friends came to support the widow: the two other directors of Patrick's firm of glass manufacturers and old Mrs. Prynne.

Tamsin wore a black dress and a large hat of glossy black straw. Throughout the service she clung to Oliver Gage's arm. On her other side Nancy, sweating in the charcoal worsted she had bought for her February honeymoon, sat with a handkerchief ready. But she never had to hand it to Tamsin who sat rigid and dry-eyed.

It was only when the coffin was being lowered into the ground that a small disturbance occurred. Freda Carnaby tore herself from Mrs. Staxton's arm and, sobbing loudly, fell to her knees beside the dark cavity. As he said afterwards to Greenleaf, Marvell thought that like Hamlet she was going to leap into the grave. But nothing dramatic happened. Mrs. Staxton helped her to her feet and drew her away.

When it was all over Tamsin slung two suitcases into the back of the black and white Mini (SIN 1A) and with Queenie in the seat beside her, drove away to stay with Mrs. Prynne.

PART TWO

8

Two days later the weather broke with a noisy spectacular thunderstorm and a man died when a tree under which he was sheltering on Chantflower golf course was struck by lightning. The silly season had begun and this was national news. For the Linchester housewives kept indoors by continuous rain, it was for days the prime topic of conversation —until something more personal and sensational took over.

The young Macdonalds had taken their baby to Bournemouth; the Willises and the Millers, each couple finding in the other the perfect neighbours and friends, were cruising together in the Canaries. Tamsin was still away. With four empty houses on Linchester Nancy was bored to tears. When Oliver came home for the week-ends, tired and uneasy, he found his evening programmes mapped out for him.

Tonight the Greenleafs and Crispin Marvell were invited for coffee and drinks. Opening his sideboard, Oliver found that Nancy had laid in a stock of cheap Cyprus sherry and bottles of cocktails as variously coloured as the liquid that used to be displayed in the flagons of old-fashioned pharmacy windows. He cursed, clinging to the shreds of his pride and remembering the days that were gone.

The mantelpiece was decorated with postcards. Nancy had given pride of place to a peacock-blue panorama from Clare Miller, relegating two monochrome seascapes to a spot behind a vase. He read Sheila Macdonald's happy scrawl irascibly. Tamsin was at the seaside too, but Tamsin had sent nothing . . .

From where he stood, desultorily watching the rain, he could hear Nancy chattering to Linda Gaveston in the kitchen. Occasionally something clearly audible if not comprehensible arose above the twittering.

'I said it was dead grotty' or 'How about that, doll?' conflicted inharmoniously with Nancy's 'You are awful, Linda.'

Oliver grunted and lit a cigarette. These visits of Linda's, ostensibly made to deliver Nancy's order of tablets of soap or a packet of Kleenex, always put him in a bad temper. They invariably led to petulance on Nancy's part, to dissatisfaction and a carping envy. It amazed Oliver that a village chemist like Waller could stock such an immense and catholic variety of luxury goods, all of which at some time or another seemed so desirable to his wife and at the same time so conducive to the saving of money. The latest in Thermos flasks, automatic tea-makers, thermostatically controlled electric blankets, shower cabinets, all these had in the year they had lived on Linchester, been recommended to Nancy and coveted by her.

'It would be such a saving in the long run,' she would say wistfully of some gimmick, using the suburban colloquialisms Oliver hated.

Moreover it was surprising that behind Waller's counter there stood concealed the most expensive ranges of cosmetics from Paris and New York, scent and creams which were apparently exclusive to him and not to be found in Nottingham or, for that matter, London. He was therefore pleasantly astonished when the door had closed on Linda to see Nancy come dancing into the room, contented, gay and in a strange way, gleeful.

'What's got into you?'

'Nothing.'

'For a poor house-bound, forsaken child bride,' he said, recalling earlier complaints, 'you're looking very gay.'

Indeed she appeared quite pretty again in the honeymoon skirt and a pink sweater, not a hand-knitted one for a change but a soft fluffy thing that drew Oliver's eyes and reminded him that his wife had, after all, an excellent figure. But his words, sharp and moody, had altered her expression from open calm to secretiveness.

'Linda told me something very peculiar.'

'Really?' he said. 'Surprise me.'

She pouted.

'Not if you're going to talk to me like that.' For a moment, a transient moment, she looked just as she had when he had first seen her dancing with the man she had been engaged to. It had been such fun stealing her from him, especially piquant because the fiancé had also been Shirley's cousin. 'Nasty Oliver! I shall save it all up till the Greenleafs get here.'

'I can see,' said Oliver in his best co-respondent's voice, 'I can see I shall have to be very nice to you.'

'Very, very nice,' said Nancy. She sat on the sofa beside him and giggled. 'You are awful! It must be the country air.' But she didn't say anything after that and presently Oliver forgot all about Linda Gaveston.

When Marvell rang the door-bell she didn't bother to tidy her hair or put on fresh make-up. There was something of a bacchante about her, exhibitionistic, crudely female. Suddenly Oliver felt old. Her naiveté embarrassed him. He went to dispense drinks from his own stock, leaving the bright mean bottles in the sideboard.

Greenleaf and Bernice had barely sat down when she said brightly:

95

'Has anyone heard from Tamsin?'

Nobody had. Oliver fancied that Marvell was looking at him quizzically.

'I don't suppose she feels like writing.' Bernice was always kind and forbearing. 'It's not as if we were any of us close friends.'

'What would she have to write about?' Greenleaf asked. 'She's not on holiday.' And he began to talk about his own holiday, planned for September this year, and to ask about the Gages'.

Holidays were a sore point with Oliver who hoped to do without one altogether. He need not have worried. Nancy was obviously not going to let the subject go as easily as that.

'Poor Tamsin,' she said loudly, drowning the doctor's voice. 'Fancy being a widow when you're only twenty-seven.'

'Dreadful,' said Bernice.

'And in such—well, awkward circumstances.'

'Awkward circumstances?' said Greenleaf, drawn unwillingly from his dreams of the Riviera.

'I don't mean money-wise.' Oliver winced but Nancy went on: 'The whole thing was so funny, Patrick dying like that. I expect you'll all think I've got a very suspicious mind but I can't help thinking it was . . .' She paused for effect and sipped her gin. 'Well, it was fishy, wasn't it?'

Greenleaf looked at the floor. The legs of his chair had caught in one of the Numdah rugs. He bent down and straightened it.

'I don't know if I ought to say this,' Nancy went on. 'I don't suppose it's common knowledge, but Patrick's father . . .' She lowered her voice. 'Patrick's father committed suicide. Took his own life.'

'Oh, dear,' said Bernice comfortably.

'I really don't know who it was told me,' Nancy said. She picked up the plate of canapés and handed it to Marvell. To his shame Oliver saw that only half a cocktail onion topped the salmon mayonnaise on each of them. 'Do have a savoury, won't you?'

Marvell refused. The plate hovered.

'Somebody told me about it. Now who was it?'

'It was me,' Oliver said sharply.

'Of course it was. And Tamsin told you. I can't imagine why.'

All childish innocence, she looked archly from face to face.

Marvell said: 'I'm afraid I'm being obtuse, but I can't quite see what Patrick's father's suicide has to do with his son dying of heart failure.'

'Oh, absolutely nothing. Nothing at all. You mustn't think I was insinuating anything about Patrick. It's just that it's one of the funny circumstances. On its own it would be nothing.'

Oliver emptied his glass and stood up. He could cheerfully have slapped Nancy's face. 'I think we're boring our guests,' he said, bracketing himself with his wife and trying to make his voice sound easy. 'Another drink, Max? Bernice?' Marvell's glass was still full. 'What about you, darling?'

'Oh, really!' Nancy burst out laughing. 'You don't have to be so discreet. We're all friends. Nothing's going to go beyond these four walls.'

Oliver felt himself losing control. These people *were* discreet. Would it, after all, ruin his career, damn him as a social creature, if in front of them he were to bawl at Nancy, strike her, push out of the room?

He stared at her, pouring sherry absently until it topped over the glass and spilled on the tray.

'Damnation!' he said.

'Oh, your table!' Bernice was beside him, mopping with a tiny handkerchief.

'Linda Gaveston was here today,' Nancy said. 'She told me something very peculiar. No, I won't shut up, Oliver. I'm only repeating it because I'd be very interested in having an opinion from a medical man. You know that funny little man who's a commercial traveller? The one who lives in the chalets?'

'Carnaby,' said Marvell.

'That's right. Carnaby. The one who was so difficult at the party. Well, the day before Patrick died he came into Waller's shop and what d'you think he tried to buy?' She waited for the guesses that never came. 'Cyanide! That's what he tried to buy.'

Greenleaf stuck out his lower lip. They had only been in the house half an hour but he began to wonder how soon he could suggest to Bernice that it was time to leave. His drink tasted thin. For the first time since he had given up smoking as an example to his patients he longed for a cigarette.

'Waller wouldn't sell anyone cyanide,' he said at last.

'Ah, no,' said Nancy triumphantly, 'he didn't. But that's not the point, is it? He wanted cyanide and maybe he managed to get it . . .' She drew breath. 'Elsewhere,' she said with sinister emphasis. 'Now why did he want it?'

'Probably for killing wasps,' said Marvell. 'It's an old remedy for getting rid of wasps.'

Nancy looked disappointed.

'Linda overheard the conversation,' she said, 'and that's just what this fellow Carnaby said. He said he wanted it for wasps. Linda thought it was pretty thin.'

Thumping his fist on the table, Oliver made them all jump.

'Linda Gaveston is a stupid little trouble-maker,' he said furiously.

'I suppose that goes for me too?'

'I didn't say so,' said Oliver, too angry to care. 'But if the cap fits . . . I hate all this under-hand gossip. If you're trying to say Carnaby gave Patrick cyanide you'd better come straight out with it.' He drank some whisky too quickly and choked. 'On the other hand, perhaps you'd better not. I don't want to pay out whacking damages for slander.'

'It won't go any further. Anyway, it's my duty as a citizen to say what I think. Everyone knows Edward Carnaby had a terrific motive for getting Patrick out of the way.'

There was an appalled silence. Nancy had grown red in the face and her plump breasts rose and fell under the clinging pink wool.

'You're all crazy about Tamsin. I know that. But Patrick wasn't. He didn't care for her a bit. He was having an affair with that awful little Freda. Night after night he was round there while her brother was out at evening classes. He used to tie that great dog of theirs up to the gate. It was just a horrid sordid little intrigue.'

As much as Oliver, Greenleaf wanted to stop her. He was immeasurably grateful for Bernice's rich cleansing laughter.

'If it was just a little intrigue,' Bernice said lightly, 'it can't have been important, can it?'

Nancy allowed her hand to rest for a moment beneath Bernice's. Then she snatched it away.

'They're twins, aren't they? It means a lot, being twins. He wouldn't want to lose her. Patrick might have gone off with her.'

But the tension was broken. Marvell, who had taken a book from the fireside shelves and studied it as if it were a first edition, now relaxed and smiled. Oliver had moved over to the record player and the red glaze had left his face.

'Well, what does Max think?' Nancy asked.

How wise Bernice had been, laughing easily, refusing to catch his eye! Greenleaf didn't really want to do a Smith-King and flee at the scent of trouble. Besides Oliver had some good records, Bartok and the wonderful Donizetti he wanted to hear again.

'You know,' he said in a quiet gentle voice, 'it's amazing the way people expect the worst when a young person dies suddenly. They always want to make a mystery.' He wondered if Bernice and, for that matter Marvell, noticed how dismay was evoking his guttural accent. 'Real life isn't so sensational.'

'Fiction stranger than truth,' Marvell murmured.

'I can assure you Patrick didn't die of cyanide. You see, of all the poisons commonly used in cases of homicide cyanide is the most easily detected. The smell, for one thing . . .'

'Bitter almonds,' Nancy interposed.

Greenleaf smiled a smile he didn't feel.

'That among other things. Believe me, it's fantastic to talk of cyanide.' His hands moved expressively. 'No, please,' he said.

'Well, what do you really think, then?'

'I think you're a very pretty girl with a vivid imagination and Linda Gaveston watches too much television. I wonder if I might have some more of your excellent whisky, Oliver?'

Oliver took the glass gratefully. He looked as if he would gladly have given Greenleaf the whole bottle.

'Music,' he said, handing records to the discerning Marvell.

'May we have the Handel?' Marvell asked politely. Nancy made a face and flung herself back among the cushions.

The sound of the rain falling steadily had formed throughout the conversation a monotonous background chorus. Now, as they became silent, the music of The Faithful Shepherd Suite filled the room. Greenleaf listened to the orchestra and noted the repetition of each phrase with the appreciation of the scientist: but Marvell, with the ear of the artist *manqué*, felt the absurd skimped room transformed about him and, sighing within himself for something irrevocably lost, saw a green grove as in a Constable landscape and beneath the leaves a lover with the Pipes of Pan.

9

THE rain ceased as darkness fell and the sky cleared suddenly as if washed free of cloud. It was a night of bright white stars, so many stars that Greenleaf had to point out and admire—although he did not know their names—the strung lights of Charles's Wain and Jupiter riding in the south.

'Patines of bright gold,' said Marvell. 'Only they're not gold, they're platinum. Patines of bright platinum doesn't sound half so well, does it?'

'It's no good quoting at me,' said the doctor. 'You know I never read anything but the *B.M.J.*' He drew a deep breath, savouring the night air. 'Very nice,' he said inadequately. 'I'm glad I summoned up the energy to walk back with you.'

'It was a sticky evening, wasn't it?' Marvell went first, holding back brambles for Greenleaf to pass along the path.

'Silly little woman,' Greenleaf said, harshly for him. 'I hope Gage can stop her gossiping.'

'It could be awkward.' Marvell said no more until the path broadened and the doctor was walking abreast of him. Then suddenly, 'May I ask you something?' he said. 'I don't want to offend you.'

'You won't do that.'

'You're a doctor, but Patrick wasn't your patient.' Marvell spoke quietly. 'I asked you if I would offend you because I was thinking of medical etiquette. But—look, I'm not scandal-mongering like Nancy Gage—weren't you very surprised when Patrick died like that?'

Greenleaf said guardedly, 'I was surprised, yes.'

'Thunderstruck?'

'Like that poor fellow on the golf course? Well, no. You see a lot of strange things in my job. I thought at first Patrick had taken an overdose of sodium amytal. I'd given him an anti-histamine, two hundred milligrammes of Phenergan, and one would potentiate . . .' He stopped, loth to give these esoteric details to a layman. 'He had the sodium amytal and I advised him to take one.'

'You left the bottle with him?'

'Now, look.' Greenleaf had said he wouldn't be offended. 'Patrick wasn't a child, Howard had prescribed them. In any case, he didn't take any more. That was the first thing Glover looked for at the post-mortem.'

Marvell opened the orchard gate and Greenleaf stepped from the forest floor on to turf and the slippery leaves of wild daffodils. The petals of a wet rose brushed his face. In the darkness they felt like a woman's fingers drenched with scent.

'The first thing?' Marvell asked. 'You mean, you looked for other things? You suspected suicide or even murder?'

'No, no, no,' Greenleaf said impatiently. 'A man had died, a young, apparently healthy man. Glover had to find out what he died of. Patrick died of heart failure.'

'Everybody dies of heart failure.'

'Roughly, yes. But there were signs that the heart had been affected before. There was some slight damage.'

They had come to the back door. The kitchen smelt of herbs and wine. Greenleaf thought he could detect another less pleasant scent. Mildew. He had never seen mushrooms growing but Marvell's kitchen smelt like the plastic trays of mushrooms Bernice bought at the village store. Marvell groped for the lamp and lit it.

'Well, go on,' he said.

'If you must know,' Greenleaf said, 'Glover made some enquiries at Patrick's old school. Tamsin didn't know anything and Patrick's parents were dead. He'd never complained to Howard about feeling ill. Only went to him once.'

'May I ask if you got anything from the school?'

'I don't know if you may,' Greenleaf said severely. 'I don't know why you want to know. But if there's going to be a lot of talk . . . Glover wrote to the headmaster and he got a letter back saying Patrick had had to be let off some of the games because he'd had rheumatic fever.'

'I see. So you checked with the doctor Patrick had when he was a child.'

'We couldn't do that.' Greenleaf smiled a small, bitter and very personal smile. 'Patrick was born in Germany. His mother was German and he lived there till he was four. Glover talked to Tamsin's Mrs. Prynne. She's one of these old women with a good memory. She remembered Patrick had had rheumatic fever when he was three—very early to have it, incidentally—and that the name of his doctor had been Goldstein.'

Marvell was embarrassed.

'But Dr. Goldstein had disappeared. A lot of people of his persuasion disappeared in Germany between 1939 and 1945.'

'Stopping for a quick drink?' Marvell asked.

Five minutes passed before he said anything more about Patrick Selby. Greenleaf felt that he had been stiff and pompous, the very prototype of the uppish medical man. To restore Marvell's ease he accepted a glass of carrot wine.

The brilliance of the white globe had increased until now only the corners of the parlour remained in shadow. A small wind had arisen, stirring the curtains and moving the trailing violet and white leaves of the Tradescantia that stood in a majolica pot on the window sill. It was rather cold.

Then Marvell said: 'I was curious about Patrick.' He sat down and warmed his hands at the lamp. Greenleaf wondered if Bernice, at home in Shalom, had turned on the central heating. 'Perhaps I have a suspicious mind. Patrick had a good many enemies, you know. Quite a lot of people must be glad he's dead.'

'And I have a logical mind,' said Greenleaf briskly. 'Nancy Gage says Carnaby tried to buy cyanide. Patrick Selby dies suddenly. Therefore, she reasons, Patrick died of cyanide. But we *know* Patrick didn't die of cyanide. He died a natural death. Can't you see that once your original premise falls to the ground there's no longer any reason to doubt that? No matter how much Carnaby hated him—if he did, which I doubt—no matter if he succeeded in buying a ton of cyanide, he didn't kill Patrick with it because Patrick didn't die of cyanide. Now, just because one person appears to have a thin motive and access—possible access—to means *that were never used at all,* you start reasoning that he was in fact murdered, that half a dozen people had motives and that one of them succeeded.' He drank the carrot wine. It was really quite pleasant, like sweet Bristol Cream. 'You're not being logical,' he said.

Marvell didn't reply. He began to wind the clock delicately as if he was being careful not to disturb the sultan and his slave whose fingers rested eternally on the silent zither. When he had put the key down he blew away a money spider that was creeping across the sultan's gondola-shaped shoe. Then he said:

'Why wasn't there an inquest?'

Greenleaf answered him triumphantly. 'Because there wasn't any need. Haven't I been telling you? And that wasn't up to Glover and Howard. That's a matter for the coroner.'

'No doubt he knows his own business.'

'You don't have inquests on people who die naturally.' Greenleaf got up, stretching cold stiff legs, and changed the subject. 'How's the hay fever?'

'I've run out of tablets.'

'Come down to the surgery sometime and I'll let you have another prescription.'

But Marvell didn't come and Greenleaf saw nothing of him for several days. Greenleaf began to think that he would hear no more of Patrick's death—until surgery time on Wednesday morning.

The first patient to come into the consulting room through the green baize door was Denholm Smith-King. He was on his way to his Nottingham factory and at last he had summoned the courage to let Greenleaf examine him.

'It's nothing,' the doctor said as Smith-King sat up on the couch buttoning his shirt. 'Only a gland. It'll go down eventually.'

'Then I suppose I shall just have to lump it.' He laughed at his own joke and Greenleaf joined in politely.

'I see you've cut down on the smoking.'

He was startled and showed it, but his eyes followed the doctor's down to his own right forefinger and he grinned.

'Quite the detective in your own way, aren't you?' Greenleaf had only noticed that the sepia stains had paled to yellow and this remark reminded him of things he wanted to forget. 'Yes, I've cut it down,' Smith-King said and he gave the doctor a heavy, though friendly buffet on the back. 'You quacks, you don't know the strains a business man has to contend with. You don't know you're born,' but his hearty laugh softened the words.

'Things going better, are they?'

'You bet,' said Smith-King.

He went off jauntily and Greenleaf rang the bell for the next patient. By ten he had seen a dozen people and he asked the last one, a woman with nettle rash, if there were any more to come.

'Just one, Doctor. A young lady.'

He put his finger on the buzzer but no-one came so he began to tidy up his desk. Evidently the young lady had got tired of waiting. Then, just as he was picking up his ignition key, the baize door was pushed feebly open and Freda Carnaby shuffled in wearily like an old woman.

He was shocked at the change in her. Impatience died as he offered her a chair and sat down himself. What had become of the bright bird-like creature with the practical starched cotton dresses and the impractical shoes? Even at the funeral she had still looked smart in trim shop-girl black. Now her hair looked as if it hadn't been washed for weeks, her eyes were bloodshot and puffy and there was a hysterical downward quirk at the corner of her mouth.

'What exactly is the trouble, Miss Carnaby?'

'I can't sleep. I haven't had a proper night's sleep since I don't know how long.' She felt in the pocket of the mock-suede jacket she wore over her crumpled print dress. The handkerchief she pulled out was crumpled too. She pressed it with pathetic gentility against her lips. 'You see, I've had a great personal loss.' The linen square brushed the corner of one eye. 'I was very fond of someone. A man.' She gulped. 'He died quite recently.'

'I'm sorry to hear that.' Greenleaf began to wonder what was coming.

'I don't know what to do.'

He had observed before that it is this particular phrase that triggers off the tears, the breakdown. It may be true, it may be felt, but it is only when it is actually uttered aloud that its full significance, the complete helpless disorientation it implies, brings home to the speaker the wretchedness of his or her plight.

'Now you mustn't say that,' he said, knowing his inadequacy. 'Time does heal, you know.' The healer passing the buck, he thought. 'I'll let you have something to make you sleep.' He drew out his prescription pad and began to write. 'Have you been away yet this year?'

'No and I'm not likely to.'

'I should try. Just a few days would help.'

'Help?' He had heard that hysterical note so often but not from her and he didn't like it. 'Help a—a broken heart? Oh, Doctor, I don't know what to do. I don't know what to do.' She dropped her head on to her folded arms and began to sob.

Greenleaf went to the sink and drew her a glass of water.

'I'd like to tell you about it.' She sipped and wiped her eyes. 'Can I tell you about it?'

He looked surreptitiously at his watch.

'If it would make you feel better.'

'It was Patrick Selby. You knew that, didn't you?' Greenleaf said nothing so she went on. 'I was very fond of him.' They never say 'love', he thought, always 'very fond of' or 'devoted to'. 'And he was very fond of me,' she said defiantly. He glanced momentarily at her tear-blotched face, the rough skin. When she said out of the blue, 'We were going to be married,' he jumped.

'I know what you're going to say. You're going to say he was already married. Tamsin didn't care for him. He was going to divorce her.'

'Miss Carnaby . . .'

But she rushed on, the words tumbling out.

'She was having an affair with that awful man Gage. Patrick knew all about it. She used to meet him in London

108

during the week. Patrick knew. She said she was going to see some old friend of her grandmother's, but half the time she was with that man.'

Sympathy fought with and finally conquered Greenleaf's distaste. Keeping his expression a kindly blank, he began to fold up the prescription.

Misinterpreting his look, she said defensively:

'I know what you're thinking. But I wasn't carrying on with Patrick. It wasn't like that. We never did anything wrong. We were going to be married. And Nancy Gage is going about all over Linchester saying Edward killed Patrick because . . . because . . .' Her sobs broke out afresh. Greenleaf watched her in despair. How was he to turn this weeping hysterical woman out into the street? How stem the tide of appalling revelation?

'And the terrible thing is I know he was killed. That's why I can't sleep. And I know who killed him.'

This was too much. He shook her slightly, wiped her eyes himself and held the glass to her lips.

'Miss Carnaby, you must get a grip on yourself. Patrick died a perfectly natural death. This is certain. I know it. You'll only do your brother and yourself a lot of harm if you go about saying things you can't substantiate.'

'Substantiate?' She stumbled over the word. 'I can *prove* it. You remember what it was like at that awful party. Well, Oliver Gage went back by himself when it was all over. I saw him from my bedroom window. It was bright moonlight and he went over by the pond. He was carrying something, a white packet. I don't know what it was, but, Doctor, suppose —suppose it killed Patrick!'

Then, he got her out of the surgery, bundled her into his own car and drove her back to Linchester.

Three letters plopped through the Gage letter box when

the post came at ten. Nancy was so sure they weren't for her that it was all of half an hour before she bothered to come down from the bathroom. Instead, her hair rolled up in curlers, wet and evil-smelling with home-perm fluid, she sat on the edge of the bath waiting for the cooking timer to ping and brooding about what the letters might contain.

Two bills, she thought bitterly, and probably a begging letter from Jean or Shirley. A saturated curler dripped on to her nose. By this time the whole of the first floor of the house smelt of ammonia and rotten eggs. She would have to use masses of that air freshener stuff before Oliver came home. Still, that was a whole two days and goodness knew how many hours away. Surely Oliver would scarcely notice the smell when he saw how wonderful her hair looked, and all for twenty-five bob.

The timer rang and she began unrolling excitedly. When the handbasin was filled with a soggy mess of curlers and mushy paper she put a towel round her shoulders, a mauve one with Hers embroidered on it in white; His, the other half of the wedding present, was scrupulously kept for Oliver—and went downstairs.

The first letter she picked up was from Jean. Nancy knew that before she saw the handwriting. Oliver's first wife was their only correspondent who saved old envelopes and stuck new address labels on them. The second was almost certainly the telephone bill. It might be as well to lose that one. Now, who could be writing to her from London?

She opened the last envelope and saw the letter heading, Oliver's newspaper, Fleet Street. It was *from* Oliver. She looked again at the envelope and at the slanted stamp. To her that meant a kiss. Did it mean that to Oliver or had it occurred by chance?

'My darling . . .' That was nice. It was also unfamiliar and unexpected. She read on. 'I am wondering if you have forgiven me for my unkindness to you at the week-end. I was sharp with you, even verging on the brutal . . .' How beautifully he wrote! But that was to be expected. It was, after all, his line. 'Can you understand, my sweet, that this was only because I hate to see you cheapening yourself? I felt that you were making yourself the butt of those men's wit and this hurt me more bitterly than I can tell you. So for my sake, darling Nancy, watch your words. This is Tamsin's business and she is nothing to us . . .' Nancy could hardly believe a letter would make her so happy. '. . . She is nothing to us. We each possess one world. Each hath one and is one.' Hath, she decided, must be typing error, but the thought was there. 'The merest suggestion that I might be . . .' Then there was a bit blanked out with x's '. . . associated with a scandal of this kind has caused me considerable disquiet. We were not close friends of the Selbys . . .'

There was a great deal more in the same vein. Nancy skipped some of it, the boring parts, and lingered over the astonishing endearments at the end. She was so ecstatically happy that, although she caught sight of her elated face in the hall mirror, she hardly noticed that her hair was hanging in rats' tails, dripping and perfectly straight.

Marvell was determined to get Greenleaf interested in the circumstances of Patrick's death and he thought it would do no harm to confront him with a list of unusual poisons. To this end he had been to the public library and spent an instructive afternoon reading Taylor. He was so carried away that he was too late for afternoon surgery—his ostensible mission, he decided, would be to collect another prescription—so he picked a bunch of acanthus for Bernice and walked up to Shalom.

'Beautiful,' Bernice said. Her husband touched the

111

brownish-pink flowers. 'What are they?' Diffidently he suggested: 'Lupins or something?'

'Acanthus,' said Marvell. 'The original model for the Corinthian capital.'

Bernice filled a white stone vase with water. 'You are a mine of information.'

'Let's say a disused quarry of rubble.' The words had a bitter sound but Marvell smiled as he watched her arrange the flowers. 'And the rubble, incidentally, is being shaken by explosions. I've been sneezing for the past three days and I've run out of those fascinating little blue pills.'

Bernice smiled. 'If this is going to turn into a consultation,' she said, 'you'd better go and have a drink with Max.'

She began on the washing up and Marvell followed Greenleaf into the sitting room. Greenleaf pushed open the glass doors to the garden and pulled up chairs in the path of the incoming cooler air. The sky directly above was a pure milky blue and in the west refulgent, brazen gold, but the long shadow of the cedar tree lapped the walls of the house. The room was a cool sanctuary.

'It might be worth finding out exactly what you're allergic to, have some tests done,' the doctor said. 'It need not be hay, you know. You can be allergic to practically anything.'

Marvell hadn't really wanted to talk about himself but now, as if to give colour to his excuse, a tickle began at the back of his nose and he was shaken by a vast sneeze. When he had recovered he said slyly:

'Well, I suppose it can't kill me.'

'It could lead to asthma,' Greenleaf said cheerfully. 'It does in sixty to eighty per cent of cases if it isn't checked.'

'I asked,' said Marvell, re-phrasing, 'if an allergy could kill you.'

'No, you didn't. And I know exactly what you're getting at,

112

but Patrick wasn't allergic to wasp stings. He had one a few days before he died and the effect was just normal.'

'All right,' Marvell said and he blew his nose. 'You remember what we were talking about the other night?'

'What you were talking about.'

'What I was talking about, then. Don't be so stiff-necked, Max.'

They had known each other for two or three years now and at first it had been Dr. Greenleaf, Mr. Marvell. Then, as intimacy grew, the use of their styles had seemed too formal and Greenleaf who hadn't been to a public school baulked at the bare surname. This was the first time Marvell had called his friend by his first name and Greenleaf felt the strange warmth of heart, the sense of being accepted, this usage brings. It made him weak where he had intended to be strong.

'Suppose,' Marvell went on, 'there was some substance, perfectly harmless under normal circumstances, but lethal if anyone took it when he'd been stung by a wasp.'

Reluctantly Greenleaf recalled what Freda Carnaby had told him about the white package carried by Oliver Gage.

'Suppose, suppose. There isn't such a substance.'

'Sure?'

'As sure as anyone can be.'

'I'm bored with Chantefleur Abbey, Max, and I've a mind to do a spot of detecting—with your help. It obviously needs a doctor.'

'You're crazy,' said Greenleaf unhappily. 'I'm going to give you a drink and write out that prescription.'

'I don't want a drink. I want to talk about Patrick.'

'Well?'

'Well, since I last saw you I've been swotting up forensic medicine . . .'

'In between the sneezes, I imagine.'

113

'In between the sneezes, as you say. As a matter of fact I've been reading Taylor's *Medical Jurisprudence*.'

'Fascinating, isn't it?' Greenleaf said, in spite of himself. He added quickly: 'It won't tell you a thing about wasp stings or rheumatic fever.'

'No, but it tells me a hell of a lot about poisons. A positive Borgias' Bible. Brucine and thallium, lead and gold. Did you know there are some gold salts called Purple of Cassius? But of course you did. Purple of Cassius! There's a name to conjure death with.'

'It didn't conjure Patrick Selby's death.'

'How do you *know*? I'll bet Glover didn't test for it.'

'No, and he didn't test for arsenic or hyoscine or the botulinus bacillus, for the simple reason that there wasn't the slightest indication in Patrick's appearance or the state of the room to suggest that he might remotely have taken any of them.'

'I have heard,' Marvell said, 'that a man can die from having air injected into a vein. Now there's a very entertaining novel by Dorothy Sayers . . .'

'*Unnatural Death*.'

'So you do read detective stories!' Marvell pounced on his words.

'Only on holiday.' Greenleaf smiled. 'But Patrick hadn't any hypodermic marks.'

'Well, well,' Marvell mocked. 'Max, you're a hypocrite. How do you know Patrick hadn't any hypodermic marks unless you looked for them? And if you looked for them you must have suspected at the least suicide.'

For a few moments Greenleaf didn't answer him. What Marvell said was near the truth. He had looked and found—nothing. But had he been in possession of certain facts of which he was now cognisant, would he have acted as he had? Wouldn't he instead have tried to dissuade Howard

114

and Glover from signing the death certificate? He had done nothing because Patrick had not been his patient, because it would have been unprofessional to poach on Howard's preserves, because, most of all, Patrick had seemed a reasonably happily married man leading a quiet normal life. Happily married? Now, of course, it sounded an absurd description of the mess he and Tamsin had made for themselves, but then . . . You had to make allowances for the uninhibited way people behaved at parties, Tamsin's close dancing with Gage, Patrick's flirtation with Freda Carnaby. The possibility of murder had never crossed his mind. Why, then, had he looked? Just to fill the time, he thought, almost convincing himself, just for something to do.

And yet, as he answered Marvell, he was fully aware that he was skirting round the question.

'I looked,' he said carefully, 'before Glover began his examination. At the time there seemed nothing to account for the death. It was afterwards that Glover found the heart damage. There were no punctures on Patrick's body apart from those made by wasps. And he didn't die from wasps' stings, unless you might say he had a certain amount of shock from the stings.'

'If by that you mean the shock affected his heart, wouldn't you have expected him to have a heart attack at once, even while he was on the ladder, not three or four hours later?'

The damage caused by the rheumatic fever had been slight. Patrick must have had it very mildly. But in the absence of Patrick's parents and Dr. Goldstein, who could tell? 'Yes, I would,' Greenleaf said unhappily.

'Max, you're coming round to my way of thinking. Look, leaving the cause of death for a moment, wasn't there something very—to use Nancy's word—fishy about that party?'

'You mean the picture?'

'I mean the picture. I went upstairs to get the citronella

and there was the picture. Now, it wasn't covered up. It was in a room in Patrick's house. But he didn't know it was there. Did you see his face when he saw it?'

Greenleaf frowned. 'It was a horrible thing,' he said.

'Oh, come. A bit bloodthirsty. By a pupil of Thornhill, I should say, and those old boys didn't pull their punches. But the point is, Patrick was terrified. He couldn't have been more upset if it had been a real head in a real pool of blood.'

'Some people are very squeamish,' said Greenleaf who was always coming across them.

'About real wounds and real blood, yes. But this was only a picture. Now, I'll tell you something. A couple of weeks before he died Patrick was in my house with Tamsin and I showed them some Dali drawings I've got. They're only prints but they're much more horrifying than Salome, but Patrick didn't turn a hair.'

'So he didn't like the picture? What's it got to do with his death? He didn't die from having his head chopped off.'

'Pity,' Marvell said cheerfully. 'If he had we'd only have two-thirds of our present problem. No longer How? but simply Why? and Who?'

He got up as Bernice came in to take him on a tour of the garden.

'I need the advice of someone with green fingers.' She raised her eyebrows at their serious faces. 'Max, you're tired. Are you all right?'

'I'm fine.' He watched them go, Bernice questioning, her companion stooping towards the border plants, his head raised, listening courteously. Then Bernice went up to the fence and he saw that Nancy Gage had come into the garden next door. She evidently had some news to impart, for she was talking excitedly with a kind of feverish desire for the sound of her own voice that women have who are left too much alone. Greenleaf could only remember the last time she had looked like that, but today there was no Oliver to stop her.

His wife's voice floated back to him. 'Tamsin's home, Max.'

Was that all?

He had hardly reached the lawn and heard Bernice say, 'Should we go over?' when Nancy caught him.

'Don't look at my hair,' she said, attracting his attention to it by running her fingers through the strawy mass. 'Something went wrong with the works.'

'Did you say Tamsin was home?'

'We ought to go over, Max, and see if she's all right.'

'Oh, she's all right. Brown as a berry,' said Nancy, and she made a mock-gesture of self-reproach, protruding her teeth over her lower lip. 'There I go. Come back all I said. Oliver says I mustn't talk about the Selbys to anyone, not anyone at all because of you-know-what.'

Marvell tried to catch Greenleaf's eye and when the doctor refused to co-operate, said, 'And what are we supposed to know?'

'Oliver says I mustn't go about saying Patrick didn't die naturally because it wouldn't do him any good.' She giggled. 'Oliver, I mean, not Patrick. He wrote it in a letter so it must be important.'

'Very prudent,' said Marvell.

Greenleaf opened his mouth to say something, he hardly knew what, and closed it again as the telephone rang. When he came back to the garden Nancy had gone.

'Little boy with a big headache,' he called to Bernice. 'Boys shouldn't have headaches. I'm going to see what it's all about and I'll look in on Tamsin on my way back.'

He went to get the car and nearly ran over Edith Gaveston's dog as he was backing it out. After he had apologised

117

she picked up the Scottie and stuck her head through the car window.

'I like your new motor,' she said archaically. 'Only don't blood it on Fergus, will you?'

Fox-hunting metaphors were lost on the doctor. He made the engine rev faintly.

'I see the merry widow's back.' She pointed across The Green. At first Greenleaf saw only Henry Glide exercising his Boxer; then he noticed that the Hallows' windows had all been opened, flung wide in a way they never were when Patrick was alive. The Weimaraner was standing by the front doors, still as a statue carved from creamy marble.

'Poor girl,' he said.

'Tamsin? I thought you meant Queenie for a minute. Poor is hardly the word I'd choose. That house, the Selby business and a private income! In my opinion she's well rid of him.'

'Excuse me,' Greenleaf said. 'I must go. I have a call.' The car slid out on to the tarmac. The Scottie yapped and Edith bellowed:

'Let's hope she hasn't come back to another scandal. One's enough but two looks like . . .'

Her last words were lost in the sound of the engine but he thought she had said 'enemy action'. He had no idea what she was talking about but he didn't like it. I'm getting as bad as Marvell, he thought uneasily, compelling his eyes to the road. Then he made himself think about headaches and children and meningitis until he came to the house where the sick boy was.

10

THE dog Queenie traversed the lawn of Hallows, re-ac-
quainting herself by scent with the home she had returned to
after a fortnight's absence. She assured herself that the squir-
rels' dray still remained in the elm by the gate, that the Smith-
Kings' cat had on several occasions crossed the wattle fence
and come to the back door, and that a multitude of birds had
descended upon the currants, leaving behind them famine
and evidence that only a dog could find.

When she had visited the locked garage and peered
through the window, whining a little by now, she knew that
the man she sought was not on Hallows land. She went back
to the house, her tail quite still, and found the woman—her
woman as he had been her man—sitting in a bedroom singing and combing her hair as she sang. The dog Queenie
placed her head in the silk lap and took a little comfort from
the combings that fell upon her like thistledown.

At first Greenleaf thought that the singing came from the
wireless. But then, as he came up to the front doors, he realised that this was no professional but a girl who sang for
joy, vaguely, a little out of tune. He rang the bell and
waited.

Tamsin was browner than he had ever seen her and he
remembered someone saying that Mrs. Prynne lived at the
seaside. She wore a bright pink dress of the shade his mother

119

used to call a wicked pink and on her arms black and white bangles.

'I came,' he said, very much taken aback, 'to see if there was anything I could do.'

'You could come in and have a drink with me,' she said and he had the impression she was deliberately crushing the gaiety from her voice. She had put on weight and she looked well. The harsh colour suited her. 'Dear Max.' She took both his hands. 'Always so kind.'

'I saw you were back,' he said as they came into the lounge. 'I've been to see a patient in the village and I thought I'd look in. How are you?'

'I'm fine.' She seemed to realise this was wrong. 'Well, what is it you people say? As well as can be expected. You've had awful weather, haven't you? It was lovely where I was. Hours and hours of sun. I've been on the beach every day.' She stretched her arms high above her head. 'Oh, Max!'

Greenleaf didn't know what to say. He looked about him at the room which Bernice used to say was like a set-piece in a furniture store or a picture in *House Beautiful*. Now it was a mess. Tamsin could scarcely have been home more than two hours but there were clothes on the sofa and on the floor, magazines and newspapers on the hearthrug. She had covered the stark mantelpiece with shells, conches, winkles, razor shells, and there was a trail of sand on the parquet floor.

'How's everyone? How's Bernice? If you've been thinking I neglected you, I didn't send a single postcard to anyone. How's Oliver? And Nancy? What have you all been doing?'

Talking, he thought, about your husband. Aloud he said:

'We've all been going on in the same way. No news. Crispin Marvell's with Bernice now giving her some tips about gardening.'

120

'Oh, Crispin.' There was scorn in her voice. 'Don't you think he rather overdoes this country thing of his?' She caught his astonished eye. 'Oh, I'm being mean, I know. But I just don't care about anyone any more—not you and Bernice, Max—I mean the others. The first thing I'm going to do is sell this place and go far far away.'

'It's a nice house,' he said for something to say.

'Nice?' Her voice trembled. 'It's like a great hothouse without any flowers.' He had never thought her mercenary and he was surprised when she said, 'I ought to get eight or nine thousand for it. Then there's the Selby business.'

'What exactly . . . ?'

'Oh, glass,' she said vaguely. 'Test tubes and things like that. It never did terribly well until recently. But a couple of months ago they got a marvellous contract making stuff for Harwell. The money's rolling in. I don't know whether to stay or sell out to the other directors. Really, Max, I'm quite a rich woman.'

There were such a lot of things he longed to ask her but could not. Where, for instance, if the business hadn't been doing well, had the money come from to buy Hallows? Why had Patrick's father committed suicide? What of Oliver Gage? And why, most of all, was she a widow of three weeks' standing, singing for joy when she returned to the house where Patrick had died? It struck him suddenly that in their conversation, so intimately concerned with him, resulting as it did, solely from his death, she had never once mentioned his name.

She took a shell from the mantelpiece and held it to her ear. 'The sound of the sea,' she said and shivered. 'The sound of freedom. I shall never marry again, Max, never.' Freedom, he thought, unaware he was quoting Madame Roland, what crimes are committed in your name!

'I must go,' he said.

'Just a minute, I've something to show you.'

She took his hand in her left one and he sensed at the back of his mind that there was an unfamiliar bareness something missing. But he forgot about it as they entered the dining room. The french windows were open and beyond them the wicker furniture on the patio was damp from many rains. This room, he remembered, had always been the most austere in the house, its walls painted white, its window hung with white blinds, so that it looked like a ward in a new hospital. But above the long sleek radiator there had once been a plaque of smoky blue pottery, a tiny island in an ocean of ice. It had been removed to lie rejected and dusty on the table, and in its place hung the picture that had frightened Patrick, dominating the room and emphasising its barrenness by contrast with its own crusted gilt, its blue and gold and bloody scarlet.

'The gardener was here when I got back,' Tamsin said. 'He helped me to hang it. Too absurd, but I thought he was going to be sick.' She smiled and stroked the mother-of-pearl conch. His gaze, withdrawn for a moment from Salome, followed the movement of her hand and he saw what he had sensed. Tamsin had discarded her wedding ring.

'She always seems to be looking at you,' Tamsin said, 'like the Mona Lisa.'

It was true. The painter had contrived that Salome's eyes should meet yours, no matter in what part of the room you were standing.

'Is it valuable?' he asked, thinking of the thousands rich men would pay for monstrosities.

'Oh, no. Mrs. Prynne said it's only worth about twenty pounds.'

She was still looking at the picture but with neither gloating nor horror. As he turned curiously to look at her he thought he saw in her eyes only the same pride of possession one of his sons might feel for a tape recorder or an electric guitar. One woman's meat, one man's poison . . .

'Patrick . . .' he tried to begin, but he could not speak the name aloud to her.

'What's the matter, darling? Not the little boy?'
'No, no, he'll be all right. I'm looking in again tomorrow.'
'You've been so long.'

Instead of sitting down Greenleaf began to pace the room. The circumstances of Patrick's death were beginning to worry him a lot. If in fact there were sufficient grounds to suspect homicide, wasn't it his duty as the first medical man to have seen Patrick's body, as one of those present at the post-mortem, to see justice done? And if he only suspected shouldn't he, as discreetly as possible, probe just enough to discover whether suspicion was well-founded? Some of the information he had was given in confidence and he couldn't tell Marvell about it. But there was one person he could tell, one from whom he had never felt it necessary to keep the secrets of the consulting room. He could tell his wife.

Bernice might well laugh away his fears and this, he had to confess, was what he wanted. She would tell him he was tired, that he needed his holiday.

The television was on, dancers in some grotesque ballet gyrating like demons. He touched the knob. 'D'you want this?' She shook her head. He switched it off and told her.

She didn't laugh but said thoughtfully:
'Tamsin and Oliver. Yes, I can believe that.'
'You can?'
'I couldn't help noticing the way they danced together at Tamsin's party. I never thought Tamsin and Patrick were very happy together. Except—except until a few days before he died. It was when I called on them collecting for the

Cancer Campaign. Tamsin kept calling Patrick darling—she was very sweet to him. I remember thinking how odd it was.'

'But apparently Patrick was in love with Freda Carnaby. Freda Carnaby after Tamsin?'

Bernice lit a cigarette and said shrewdly, 'Did you ever notice how very teutonic Patrick was? The first four years of his life must have influenced him a lot. Of course, his mother was German. He was an awfully *kinder, küche, kirche* sort of person, house-proud, passionately neat and tidy. But Tamsin's a sloppy girl. Not in her appearance, she's vain about that, but about the house. You could see it narked Patrick.'

Greenleaf's mind went back half an hour. Again he saw the untidy rooms, the shells dribbling sand.

'Now, Freda Carnaby, she'd be different again. Very brisk and practical—or she used to be. All the time they've been here I've never seen her in slacks or without stockings, Max. Time and time again I've noticed it, women who wear those tight little pointed shoes are mad keen on polishing and turning out rooms. Patrick was cruel, too, you know, Max, but I don't think cruelty would get very far with Tamsin. She's too vague and self-sufficient. But Freda Carnaby! There's a masochist if ever I saw one.'

'You may be right,' Greenleaf said. 'But forget the Carnabys for a minute. What about Gage? I can imagine he might want to marry Tamsin.' He grinned faintly. 'He has marriages like other people have colds in the head. But apparently Patrick was going to divorce Tamsin anyway. Would Gage want to'—He almost baulked at the word—'to *kill* him?'

Bernice said unexpectedly, 'He's rather a violent man.'

'Violent? Oliver Gage?'

'Nancy told me something when they first came here. I

didn't repeat it because I know how you hate that kind of thing. She was proud of it.'

'So?'

'Well, when Oliver first met her she was engaged to some relative of his second wife's. Apparently Oliver just set out to get her. It's a strange way of conducting one's life, isn't it? Oliver and the fiancé were playing billiards in Oliver's house and Nancy came in. Anyway, the fiancé said something to her she didn't like and she told him she'd finished with him and that she was going to marry Oliver. Just like that. Oliver and the fiancé had a violent quarrel and the upshot of it was Oliver hit him over the head with a billiard cue.'

Greenleaf smiled incredulously.

'It isn't really funny, Max. He knocked the fellow out cold.'

'Hitting someone over the head is a long way from poisoning a man in cold blood. Freda Carnaby says she saw him carrying a packet. A packet of what? Glover was very thorough in his tests.' He sighed. 'I've never been interested in toxicology. When I was a student I didn't care much for medical jurisprudence. But I always come back to that in the end. If Patrick was killed, what was he killed with?'

'One of those insecticides?' Bernice asked vaguely. 'You know, you read about them in the papers. I thought they weren't supposed to leave any trace.'

'Not in the body maybe. But there would have been signs. He would have been very sick. The sheets on the bed, Bernice, they weren't clean sheets. I don't mean they were dirty —just not fresh on.'

'Observant of you,' said Bernice. She reached for the cigarettes, caught her husband's eye and let her hand drop.

'Besides, why would Gage want to do away with Patrick? There's always divorce. Unless he couldn't afford two

125

divorces. He'd have to pay the costs of both of them, remember.'

'On the other hand, Tamsin has her private income.'

Greenleaf banged his fist on the chair arm.

'Wherever I go I keep hearing about that private income. What does it amount to, I'd like to know. Hundreds? Thousands? A couple of hundred a year wouldn't make any difference to a man in Oliver's position. Killing Patrick would secure his money too and that might pay for Nancy's divorce. And Tamsin . . .'

Bernice stared.

'You don't mean you think Tamsin . . . ? Would a woman murder her own husband?'

'They do, occasionally.'

She got up and stood before him. He took her hand and held it lightly.

'Don't worry,' he said. 'Maybe I do need that holiday.'

'Oh, darling, I don't want you to get into this. I'm scared, Max. This can't be happening, not here on Linchester.'

Reading her thoughts, he said gently, 'Whatever we have said no-one can hear us.'

'But we have said it.'

'Sit down,' he said. 'Listen. There's something we've got to realise. If someone did kill Patrick, Tamsin must be in it too. She was in the house. I left her and she says she went to bed. You're not going to tell me someone got into the house without her knowing?'

'You said she was happy?'

'Now? Yes, she's happy now. I think she's glad Patrick's dead. After I told her he was dead she didn't cry, but she cried later. She put her arms round the dog and she cried. Bernice, I think she was crying from relief.'

'What will you do?'

'I don't know,' he said. 'Maybe, nothing. I can't go about

asking questions like a detective.' He stopped, listening. A key turned in the lock and he heard the boys come into the hall. And if those women talk, he thought, if Nancy goes about saying Carnaby killed Patrick with cyanide and Freda says Gage killed him with a mysterious white packet, I shall begin to lose my patients.

11

'ONE large jar of zinc and castor oil cream, half a dozen packets of disposable nappies, a dozen tins of strained food . . .' Mr. Waller reckoned up the purchases rapidly. 'Gone are the days of all that mashing and fiddling about with strainers, Mrs. Smith-King. I always say you young mothers don't know how lucky you are. A large tin of baby powder and the Virol.' He handed the things to Linda who wrapped each up efficiently and sealed it with sellotape. 'I'm afraid that comes to three pounds seven and tenpence. Say it quickly and it doesn't sound so bad, eh?'

Joan Smith-King gave him a new five pound note.

'It's terrible the way it goes,' she said. 'Still, you can't expect it to be cheap taking five children away on holiday.' She jerked Jeremy's hand from its exploration of Linda's carefully arranged display of bathing caps, each an improbably coloured wig of nylon hair on a rubber scalp. 'I can't tell you how relieved I am to be going at all. My husband's had a very worrying time lately with the business but now everything's panned out well and he'll be able to take a rest.'

'There you are, Mrs. Smith-King. Three pounds, seven and ten, and two and two is ten, and ten and a pound is five pounds. Sure you can manage? What can we do for you, Mr. Marvell?'

'Just a packet of labels, please,' said Marvell who was

next in the queue. 'I'm going to start extracting honey in a day or two.' He pocketed the envelope and they left the shop together. Outside Greenleaf's car was parked against the kerb and the doctor was emerging from the newsagent's with the local paper.

'Have you seen it?' Joan Smith-King asked him. 'On the property page. You have a look.'

Greenleaf did as he was told, struggling with the pages in the breeze. The display box among the agents' advertisements wasn't hard to find: Luxury, architect-designed modern house on the favoured Linchester estate at Chantflower in the heart of rural Notts. yet only ten miles from city centre. Large lounge, dining room with patio, superb kitchen, three bedrooms, two bathrooms.

'She doesn't let the grass grow under her feet,' said Joan. 'I'll be glad to see the back of that dog, that Queenie thing. My children are scared stiff of dogs.' Jeremy listened, learning terror at his mother's knee. 'You might not believe it but Patrick Selby was all set to ruin Den's business just because he once hit that dog. I mean, really! Imagine trying to take away someone's livelihood just because he took a stick to an animal.'

Marvell said softly:

'The dog recovered from the bite, the man it was that died.'

'Now look, I didn't mean . . .' A deep flush spread unbecomingly across her lantern jaws. She stepped back. 'I'm sorry I can't give you a lift. I've got a car full of kids.'

'Come on,' Greenleaf said. He tossed the paper into the back of the car. Marvell got in beside him.

'Sorry,' he said. 'I can see you don't like my detective methods. But it's funny, nobody loved him. His wife was bored with him, he got in the way of his wife's lover—Oh, I've found out about that—his girl friend's brother was afraid of him. Even I was annoyed with him because he cut down my father's trees. Edith disliked him because he played God with her children and now you have Smith-King. I wonder what he was up to there, Max. He told me he was trying to get a Stock Exchange quotation for his shares and expand a bit. Do you suppose he had his cold fishy eye on Smith-King's little lot?'

'I'm not listening.'

'Do you happen to know what Smith-King's line is?'

'Chemicals,' Greenleaf said.

'Drugs mainly. And you realise what that means. He must have access to all kinds of lethal stuff. Or there's Linda. She works for Waller and I don't suppose she's above "borrowing" a nip of something for her mother. And what about that Vesprid stuff?'

Bernice had suggested insecticides. Doubt stirred until Greenleaf remembered how he had answered her. 'You'll have to stop all this, you know,' he said, 'Nobody could have got into the house because Tamsin was there.'

'Not all the time. After you'd gone she went out.'

'What?' Greenleaf signalled right and turned into Long Lane. 'How do you know?'

'Because she came to see me,' Marvell said.

Greenleaf had intended to drop Marvell at the almshouse and drive straight home. But Marvell's statement had suddenly put a different complexion on things. He slammed the car doors and they went up to the house.

'She came,' Marvell said, 'to bring me the currants. You remember the currants? She picked them before the party and put them in a trug.'

'A what?'

'Sorry. I keep forgetting you're not a countryman. It's a kind of wooden basket, a gardener's basket. In all the fuss

I forgot them and Tamsin brought them up to me. It must have been all of midnight.'

Midnight, Greenleaf thought, and she walked through those woods alone. She came down here while Patrick—if not, as far as anyone then knew, dying—was at least ill and in pain. She came to bring a basket of currants! It was no good, he would never understand the habits of the English countryside. But Tamsin was accustomed to them. She had learnt in these two years as much from Marvell as she would have from a childhood spent among the fields and hedgerows.

'I was sitting at the window reading through my stuff and I saw her in the orchard.' Marvell knelt down to tie up a hollyhock that the wind had blown adrift from the porch wall. Greenleaf watched him smooth the stem and press back the torn green skin. 'She looked like a moth or a ghost in that dress. Patrick didn't like bright colours. She was carrying the trug and that straw handbag Edith Gaveston gave her for a birthday present. I was—well, somewhat surprised to see her.' He straightened up and stepped into the porch. Greenleaf fancied that he was embarrassed, for, as he lifted the can and began watering the pot plants that stood on the shelves, he kept his face turned away.

'She came all this way to give you some currants?'

Marvell didn't answer him. Instead he said:

'It means, of course, that anyone could have got into the house. Nobody around here bothers to lock their doors except you and Bernice. I walked back with her as far as her gate.' He stroked a long spear-shaped leaf and, wheeling round suddenly, said fiercely: 'My God, Max, don't you think I realise? If I'd gone in I might have been able to do something.'

'You couldn't know.'

'And Tamsin . . . ?'

'Thought he was asleep,' he said, voicing a confidence he didn't feel. 'Why did she really come?'

Marvell was touching with the tips of his fingers a dark green succulent plant on the borders of whose leaves tiny leaflets grew.

'The Pregnant Frau,' he said. 'You see, she grows her children all round the edges of her leaves and each one will grow into another plant. They remind me of the leaves in Jacobean embroidery. And this one . . .' He fingered the spear-shaped plant, '. . . is the Mother-in-law's Tongue. You see I keep a harem in my porch.'

'Why did she come?'

'That,' Marvell said, 'is something I can't really tell you.' Greenleaf looked at him, puzzled as to whether he meant he refused to tell him or was unable to do so. But Marvell said no more and presently the doctor left him.

He hadn't meant to go back to the village and into Waller's shop. He *meant* to turn off at the Manor gates, but something impelled him on down the hill, unease perhaps, or the knowledge that Tamsin had left Patrick alone on the night he died.

'I want a tin of Vesprid,' he said, cutting short Waller's obsequious greeting. Instead of calling for Linda, Waller got it down himself.

'I suppose I shall have to wear gloves and a mask,' Greenleaf said innocently.

'Absolutely harmless to warm-blooded . . .' Waller's voice trailed away. In this company, and only then, was his confidence shaken. A small voice within his heart told him that to Greenleaf, Howard and their partners, he could never be more than the village medicine man. 'At least . . . well, I don't have to tell *you*, Doctor.'

When he got home Greenleaf transferred some of the

liquid into a small bottle and wrapped it up. It was far-fetched, incredibly far-fetched, to imagine Edward Carnaby going back to Hallows after the party, to wonder if Freda's story of Gage and the white packet was a cover-up for her brother's own trip with a tin of insecticide. Or was it? He went back to the car, drove to the post office and sent the package away to be analysed.

12

THE Chantflower Rural Council dustmen hadn't bargained on the extra load of rubbish that awaited them outside the Hallows back door. They grumbled loudly, muttering about slipped discs and no overtime. Queenie stood on the steps and roared at them.

'Now, if you'll just take these over to Mrs. Greenleaf I'll give you a shilling,' said Tamsin to Peter Smith-King. He was only ten and he looked dubiously at the two suitcases. 'The money'll be useful for your holiday. Come on, they're not really heavy and you can make two journeys. Tell her they're for Oxfam.'

The little boy hesitated. Then he went home and fetched his box barrow. He trundled the cases across the Green, dawdling to throw a stone at the swans, and found Bernice on the lawn giving coffee to Nancy Gage and Edith Gaveston.

'Can we have a peep?' Nancy asked. Without waiting for permission she undid the clasps on the larger case. The lid fell back to reveal, on top of a pile of clothes, a straw hand-bag embroidered with raffia.

'Oh, dear!' Nancy said.

Edith blushed.

'Of course, I could see she didn't like it,' she said. 'She barely said two words to me when I gave it to her, but really!'

'There's such a thing as tact,' Nancy said happily.

Edith snatched the bag and opened it.

134

'She hasn't even bothered to take the tissue paper out.'

'Goodness,' Nancy giggled, 'I don't know what use she thinks a handbag is to a starving Asian.' And her eyes goggled as she imagined an emaciated peasant clutching Edith's present against her rags.

'The clothes will be useful though,' Bernice said pacifically.

Nancy stared in horrified wonder as the doctor's wife lifted from the case the slacks and tee-shirt Patrick had worn on the evening of his death. For all their careful laundering they suggested a shroud.

Nancy was on her knees now, unashamedly burrowing. 'Two suits, shoes, goodness knows how many shirts.' She unfastened the other case. 'All Patrick's clothes!'

'Now if it were Paul....' Edith began to describe minutely exactly how she would dispose of her husband's effects in the event of his death. While she was talking Bernice quietly sealed the cases and re-filled the coffee pot.

Returning after a few moments, she was aware from Nancy's expression that the conversation had taken a different and more exciting turn. The two women under the cedar tree wore ghoulish lugubrious looks. As she approached she caught the words 'very unstable' and 'a most peculiar family altogether'.

How difficult it was to close one's ears to gossip, how impossible to reprimand friends! Bernice sat down again, listening but not participating.

'Of course I don't know the details,' Nancy was saying.

'Black, please, Bernice,' Edith said. 'Well, that Mrs. Selby—I mean Patrick's mother—it gets so confusing, doesn't it? That Mrs. Selby ran away with another man. We used to call it bolting when I was a girl.' She pronounced it 'gel', snapping her tongue wetly from the roof of her mouth. 'Apparently they'd always been most happily married,

married for years. Patrick was grown up when she went off. She must have been all of fifty, my dear, and the man was older. Anyway, she persuaded Patrick's father to divorce her and he did, but . . .'

'Yes?' Nancy's forlorn, ghoulish face would have deceived no-one. Her mouth was turned down but her bright eyes flickered.

'But on the day she got her decree Patrick's father gassed himself! '

'No! '

'My dear, it was a terrible scandal. And that wasn't all. Old Mrs. Selby, the grandmother—Tamsin's grandmother, too. Dreadful this in-breeding. Look what it does to dogs! She made a terrible scene at the inquest and shouted that her son would still be alive but for the divorce.'

Bernice moved her chair into the shade. 'You're romancing, Edith. You can't possibly know all this.'

'On the contrary. I know it for certain.' Edith drew herself up, the lady of the manor making her morning calls. 'It so happens I read the account of the inquest in *The Times*. It stuck in my mind and when Nancy mentioned the suicide it all came back to me. Selby, a glass factory. There's no doubt about it being the same one.'

'It's all very sad.' Bernice looked so repressive that Nancy jumped up, scattering biscuit crumbs.

'I must love you and leave you. Oh, Bernice, I nearly forgot to ask you. Have you got the name of that man who put up your summer house?'

'I can't remember. Max would know.'

Nancy waited for her to ask why. When she didn't she said proudly:

'We're going to have that extension done at last, but Oliver says Henry Glide's a bit too pricey. A sun loggia. . . .' She paused. 'And a pram park! '

'Nancy, you're not. . . .? How lovely! '

Nancy pulled in her waist and laughed.

'No, not yet,' she said, 'but Oliver says we can go in for a baby any time I like.'

Trying not to smile at the ludicrous phrase, Bernice found herself saying once more that it was lovely.

'He's been as nice as pie about it and he's all over me. He hasn't been so lovey-dovey for months. Aren't men the end?'

I really ought to thank Tamsin properly for the clothes, Bernice thought after they had both gone. But she felt reluctant to go. Hardly anyone had set eyes on Tamsin since her return. She had become like a sleeping beauty shut up in her glass castle, or like a lurking witch. Bernice couldn't make up her mind whether Tamsin was really bad or whether the gossip had created in her own fancy an unreal Tamsin, a false clever poisoner. Anyway, she must go and be polite.

As she hurried across The Green she encountered Peter sitting on his barrow.

'I went to collect my shilling,' he said, 'but I couldn't find *her*.' He picked up a flat stone and concentrated on sending it skimming across the water. 'The dog's there, though.'

He threw this piece of information out quite casually but Bernice remembered what Max had told her and detected a current of fear.

'I'm on my way over now,' she said. 'Come with me if you like.'

Queenie was indeed there so Tamsin must be too. As she put out her hand to the dog's soft mouth Bernice had a strange feeling that something ought to click. When Tamsin went out without the dog she always shut her in the kitchen. The Weimaraner had been bred as a sentinel as well as a hunter. What was it Max had said last night about Tamsin visiting Crispin Marvell? She stopped and pondered. Tamsin's voice from above broke into her reverie.

'Come on in. I was in the bath.'

Peter slunk past the dog.

'Go into the dining room. I won't be a minute.'

Bernice pushed open the double doors and Peter went in first. The dining room door was just ajar. Peter went obediently ahead but Bernice waited in the hall. The last thing she wanted was to stay and talk.

She expected Peter to sit down and wait for his wages but he didn't. He stopped and stared at something. She could see nothing inside the room but the child's figure in profile, still as a statue. Then he came out of the room again, backing from whatever it was like someone leaving the presence of royalty. He looked at her and she saw that his face was white but stoical.

'Ughugh,' he said.

At once she knew what he had seen. Surely nothing else Tamsin possessed could summon that squeamish pallor even in a child of ten. She closed the door firmly and turned round. A gasp escaped her before she could control it. Tamsin was behind her, awfully near, clean and gleaming as a wax doll in her pink and white dressing gown. Suddenly Bernice felt terribly frightened. Tamsin had come so silently, the child was silent and now all the doors were closed.

'What's the matter with him?'

If he had been her own child Bernice would have put her arms around him and pressed his grubby cheek against her face. But she could give him no physical comfort. He was too old to hug and too young for explanations.

She felt her voice quiver and jerk as she said, 'I think he saw that picture of yours'.

'Too uncanny,' said Tamsin. She looked at Peter as if

138

she were seeing not him but another child staring out through his eyes. 'Patrick was just about your age when he first saw it, but he wasn't tough like you. He ran away and then *it* happened. The fuss and bother—you can't imagine.'

Bernice was just going to ask what had happened when Peter said sullenly, 'Can I have my shilling?'

'Oh, of course you can. It's there, all ready for you on the table.'

The moment of revelation had passed. Tamsin evidently thought Bernice had come to give Peter moral support, for she opened the door to show them both out.

'I only came to thank you for the things.'

'So glad they're useful. And now I must chase you both away. I've got people coming to look over the house.'

Edith was the first person on Linchester to find out that Hallows was sold and she got it from the gardener the Gavestons shared with Tamsin. As soon as he had told her, over mid-morning tea in the utility room, she slipped out to pass the news on to Mrs. Glide. Henry, after all, ought to be pleased that his handiwork found favour in the sight of buyers. On her way back she met Marvell returning from the shops with his sparse groceries in a string bag.

'Only yesterday, it was,' she said, 'and they made an offer on the spot. These *noveaux riches*, they buy and sell houses like you or Paul might job in and out on the stock market.'

Marvell pursed his lips, listening gravely.

'Now when we were young a house *was* a house. One's grandfather had lived in it and in the fulness of time one's grandson would live in it too.' She ended with sublime insensitivity, 'It was *there*, like the Rock of Ages'.

He smiled, murmured something, his mind working furiously. So Tamsin was leaving soon, escaping . . . When

Edith had left him he walked slowly across The Green towards Shalom. He tried the front door and the back. Both were locked. The Greenleafs were townspeople, fearful of burglars, cautious people who yet declared their absence with fastened bolts and conspicuously closed windows. Marvell scribbled a note on the grocer's chit and left it on the back doorstep weighted down with a stone.

Greenleaf found it when he came in at one.

'Can you drop in this afternoon?' he read. 'I've something to tell you. C.M.'

He suppressed a sigh. Tamsin would soon be gone and with her departure surely the rumours would cease. In a fortnight's time he would be off on holiday and when he came back Nancy would be too preoccupied with plans for the baby, Freda too tranquillised by drugs to bother about the vanished Selbys. And yet, he thought as he began to eat the cold lunch Bernice had left him, Marvell might want him for something quite different. In the past he had often been summoned to give an emergency injection of piriton when Marvell was almost numbed and blinded by hay fever. Without a telephone, Marvell was obliged to call or leave a note. It was even possible that he wanted to show the doctor his manuscript, perhaps finished at last. 'I've something to tell you . . .' Patrick. He could only mean Patrick. Probably another undetectable poison theory. Well, it was a way of passing his free afternoon.

As he washed his plate and stuck it in the rack to drain, he thought with the small grain of superiority he allowed himself, that when people spoke of the rewards of a medical vocation they ignored this one: the pleasure of shooting the layman's theories down in flames.

On the wooden bench by the back door Marvell sat reading a recipe for ratafia. It was an old recipe, part of a collection his mother had made while still chatelaine of Linchester, and it had been handed down to her, mother to daughter, from a long line of forbears. Brandy, peach kernels, sugar, honey, orange flower water . . . He had no peaches, nor the money to buy them. The recipe said five hundred kernels and, basking in the warm soft sunlight, he imagined with some delight the preliminary labour to the making of ratafia: the consumption of those five hundred ripe peaches.

Presently he got up and began to walk around the house, touching the bricks, themselves peach-coloured. When he came to the side wall where Henry Glide had discovered the fissure, the terrible sign that the whole building was beginning to subside, he closed his eyes and saw only a red mist filled with whirling objects. Then, because he refused to deny facts and deceive himself, he forced his fingers to seek the crack as a man fearful of cancer yet resolute, compels his hand to probe the swelling in his body.

He jumped when Greenleaf coughed behind him.

'Penny for your thoughts.'

'They're worth more than that,' Marvell said lightly. 'To be precise, a thousand pounds.'

Greenleaf looked at him inquiringly.

'That,' said Marvell, 'is the price Glide is prepared to pay me for this land.'

'You're selling? But this place—I thought you were so fond of it.' Greenleaf described with splayed fingers a wide arc that embraced the squat yet elegant house, the shaven lawn, the orchard and the hawthorn hedge over which honeysuckle climbed, a parasite more lovely than its prey. All this meant little to the doctor but by a terrific effort of empathy he had learned its value to his friend. Even he who could scarcely tell a lily from a rose, felt that here the air smelled more sweetly and the sun's heat was moderated to a mellow beneficence. 'The house. It's so old. It's quaint.' He added helplessly, 'People like that sort of thing. They'd want to buy it.'

Marvell shook his head. He was still holding the recipe book and slowly the thought formed in his mind: I will make some ratafia, just a very small quantity, to take away and to remind me. . . .

Aloud he said to Greenleaf: 'It's falling down. The council says it's not safe to live in. I've had Glide here to look at it and all he said was he'd give me a thousand for the land.'

'How long have you known?'

'Oh, about a month now. A thousand's good going, you know. When the Marvells had Andreas Quercus—he was really called Andrew Oakes or something—when they had him build this place for four old persons of the parish of Chantflower, they didn't care that you could only get to it down a muddy lane and the old persons were too grateful to care.'

With what he felt to be tremendous inadequacy, Greenleaf said: 'I'm sorry. Where will you live?' So many questions leapt to his mind, Have you any money? What will you live on? He couldn't dream of asking them. The proximity of Linchester made poverty a more than usually shameful thing.

'I suppose I can get a room somewhere. I can teach. I shall have my thousand pounds. You'd be surprised what a long time I can live on a thousand pounds.' He laughed dryly and Greenleaf, seeing him in the light of this new knowledge, noticed how gaunt he was. This, then, was why Marvell had sent for him, to unburden his soul. I wonder, he thought, if I could rake up a bit, just to tide him over and have the place made watertight. But Marvell's next words temporarily banished all thoughts of a loan.

'I saw Edith this morning,' he said, 'as I was coming back

142

from the village. She said Tamsin had sold the house. Some people came and made her an offer.'

'Then she'll soon be gone,' said Greenleaf, relieved.

'And since perhaps neither of us will ever see her again I think I can tell you why she came to see me on the night Patrick died.'

He could see her now as she had come up through the orchard, swinging her basket, all pale in the moonlight with her mist-coloured dress, and paler still when she came within the radiance of his lamp. To his fanciful imagination the currants had seemed like beads of white jade veined with crimson. For all her affected speech, the superlatives that came from her lips so often that they lost their meaning and their force, her face had always been a mask, a shield deliberately maintained to hide intellectual cunning or perhaps a chance trick of nature concealing only vacuity.

'I think she is really very clever,' he said to Greenleaf.

He had put his head out of the window and called to her, then gone into the garden and asked after Patrick.

'Oh, Patrick—he spoiled my lovely party. Maddening creature.'

'You shouldn't have come all this way alone. I would have come up tomorrow.'

'Crispin darling, how should I know what you do here in your enchanted cottage? You might have wanted to make your wine tonight at some special witching hour.'

'I'll walk back with you.'

But she had unlatched the door already and pulled him after her into the little damp kitchen. The scent of the night came in with her and as for a moment she stood beside him, very close with her face uplifted, he could smell the richer perfume she wore, Nuit de Beltane, exotic, alien to an

143

English garden. This essence with its hint of witchcraft enhanced the atmosphere of magic unreality.

'So we sat down,' he said, shaking his shoulders as if to shed a memory. 'We sat a long way from each other but the lamp was between us and you know what oil lamps are. They seem to enclose you in a little snug circle. For a while we talked the usual trivia. Then, quite suddenly, she began to talk about us.'

'You and herself?'

'Yes. She said what a lot we had in common, how we both loved country things. She said there had always been a kind of bond between us. Max, I felt very uneasy.'

'And then?'

'I want you to understand how curiously intimate the whole situation was, the darkness around us, the circle of light. After a while she got up and sat beside me on the footstool. She took my hand and said she supposed I realised she hadn't been happy with Patrick for a long time. She's got one of those thick skins that can't blush, but I felt the blush was there.'

'Everyone can blush,' said the doctor.

'Well, be that as it may, she went on to tell me she knew why I came to the house so often. I didn't say a word. It was horribly awkward. She kept hold of my hand and she said she'd only realised how I felt when I brought her the mead and the roses. Max, believe me, they were just presents for a pretty woman from a man who can't afford scent or jewellery.'

'I believe you.'

'Suddenly she said very abruptly: "Patrick's leaving me. He wants a divorce. In a year I'll be free, Crispin." It was a blunt proposal of marriage.' Marvell went on quickly: 'I don't want marriage. For one thing I can't afford it. Everybody thinks I'm comfortably off, but the fact is most of the

144

money my father got for Linchester went in death duties. What was left was divided between my brother, my sister and myself and my share went on buying the almshouses. The family had sold them long ago. But I couldn't tell Tamsin all that. I felt she might offer me her own money.'

'That mysterious private income,' Greenleaf said.

'Not mysterious. It amounts to about fifty thousand pounds—the capital, that is—but Tamsin can't touch that. It's invested in oil or something and she has the income for life. I believe it would pass to her children, if she ever had any children. So, you see, I couldn't talk about money to her. Instead I said I was too old for her. I'm fifty, Max. She has a lot of natural dignity, but I thought she was going to cry. I don't mind telling you, it was the most embarrassing experience of my life. I suppose I was weak. I said quite truthfully that she was the most beautiful and the most exciting woman I knew. Then I said, "Wait till the year is up. I'll come and see if you've changed your mind." But she only laughed. She got up and stood outside the lamplight and said quite coolly, "Patrick will probably name Oliver Gage. I've been having an affair with him. Did you know?" I realised she was telling me I'd be taking Gage's leavings.'

'And that was all?'

'That was all, or nearly all. I tipped the currants into a bowl and walked back with her, carrying the empty trug. All the way back she was utterly silent and at the gate I left her.'

'Did you see anyone?'

'No-one. It was all so extraordinary, like a dream. But the most extraordinary thing was when I saw her the day after Patrick died, the next day. I didn't want to go, Max, but I felt I should. She was as cold as ice. Not miserable, you understand; the impression she gave me was of happiness and freedom. She might never have come to see me the night before. Then, when she came back, I met her out with

Queenie in Long Lane. She waved to me and said hallo. I asked her how she was and she said fine. I'm selling up and leaving as soon as I can. It was as casual as if we'd never been more than acquaintances.'

'Peculiar,' Greenleaf said.

'I don't mind telling you,' Marvell said with a smile, 'it was a hell of a relief.'

PART THREE

13

Two days later Marvell began extracting honey. Greenleaf's jar would be ready for him in the afternoon, he told the doctor, if he cared to come along and collect it. But at half-past three Greenleaf was still sitting in his deck-chair under the shade of the cedar tree. Bernice had gone out and he was half-asleep. Each time he nodded off, snatches of dreams crept upon him, bright pictures rather than actual episodes. But they were not pleasant images and they mirrored a subconscious of which he had been unaware. Worst of all was the hideous cameo of Tamsin's painting that spiralled and enlarged, twisted and distorted until the head on the plate became Patrick's. He jolted out of sleep to a shrill insistent ringing. Consciousness, reality, came back as with the familiar feel of the canvas, the cool springy grass, he sought tranquillity. Almost in the past days he had found peace of mind. Was it all there still below the surface, a whirlpool of fear and doubt and indecision? The ringing continued and he was suddenly aware that this was not a sound within his head, but the peal of a real bell, the telephone bell.

Reminding himself that he was supposed to be on call, he hastened into the morning room. It was Edward Carnaby.

'I thought I wasn't going to get you,' he said reproachfully. 'It's my Cheryl, my daughter. A wasp got her on the lip,

149

Doctor. Her and Freda, they were having a bit of a picnic on The Green and this wasp was on a piece of cake . . .'

'Her lip?' From Patrick, Greenleaf's thoughts travelled back to the dead miner. 'Not inside her mouth?'

'Well, sort of. Inside her lip. She's scared stiff. Mind you, Freda's had something to do with that. They're both sobbing their hearts out.'

'All right, I'll come.'

'I thought we'd seen the last of those wasps,' he said as he walked into the Carnaby lounge. Of course it was the only living room they had but it seemed strange to him to cover the entire centre of the carpet with what looked like a dismantled internal combustion engine spread on sheets of newspaper.

'You'll have to excuse the mess,' Carnaby said, blackening his fingers in his haste to remove obstacles from the doctor's path. 'I borrowed it from the class. I can't seem to . . .'

'Never mind all that!' Freda was on the sofa, squeezing the child in a vice-like hug against her fussy starched blouse. Greenleaf picked his way over to her, stepping gingerly across coils and wheels. He thought he had seldom seen anyone look so tense. Her mouth was set as if she was grinding her teeth and the tears poured down her cheeks. 'Tell me quickly, Doctor, is she going to die?'

Cheryl struggled and began to howl.

'Of course she isn't going to die,' Greenleaf said roughly while Carnaby fumbled at his feet with bits of metal.

'She is, she is! You're just saying that. You'll take her to the hospital and we'll never see her again.'

He was surprised at so much emotion for she had never seemed to care for the child. Patrick's death must have left a real wound into which a new-found maternal love might pour. Patrick, always back to Patrick . . . He looked quickly at Carnaby, wondering when the report would come from the analyst, before saying sharply to Freda:

'If you can't control yourself, Miss Carnaby, you'd better go outside.'

She gulped.

'Let's have a look at it, Cheryl.' He prised Freda off her and gently eased the handkerchief from her mouth. The lower lip was bulging into a grotesque hillock and it reminded the doctor of pictures he had seen of duck-billed women. He wiped her eyes. 'You're going to have a funny face for a day or two.'

The child tried to smile. She edged away from her aunt and pushed tendrils of hair from her big characterful eyes, eyes that she must surely have inherited from her mother.

'Mr. Selby had wasp stings,' she said and darted a precocious glance at Freda. 'I heard Daddy talking about it when they got back from that party. I was awake. I never sleep when I have a sitter.' Her lip wobbled. 'It was that Mrs. Staxton. She said wasps were ever so dangerous and she was scared of them, so Daddy said he'd got some stuff and she could take the tin. And she did, she took it home with her and a jolly good thing, because wasps *are* dangerous.' Greenleaf sighed with silent relief. The analyst's report could hardly matter now. Cheryl's voice rose into fresh panic. 'Mr. Selby *died*. Aunty Free said I might die.'

Greenleaf felt in his pocket for a sixpence.

'There's an ice-cream man by The Green,' he said. 'You'll catch him if you hurry. You get a lolly.' Carnaby looked at him, a foolish smile curling his mouth uneasily as if at some inconsequential joke. 'It'll be good for your lip.'

Freda watched her go with tragic eyes. She evidently thought Greenleaf had got rid of Cheryl in order to impart confidential information as to her probable fate. She looked affronted when he said instead:

'Patrick Selby did *not* die of wasp stings. I thought you had more sense, Miss Carnaby. To talk of dying to a child of eight! What's the matter with you?'

'Everybody knows Patrick didn't die of heart failure,' she said stubbornly.

Greenleaf let it pass. Her bosom quivered. The fallen tears had left round transparent blotches on the thin blouse through which frilly fussy straps and bits of underclothes showed.

'He must have died of the stings,' she insisted, 'and he only had four.'

'Five, but it doesn't matter. Cheryl . . .'

'He didn't. He only had four I was sitting with him and I could see.'

Greenleaf said impatiently:

'I should give that a rest, Miss Carnaby.'

Carnaby who had remained silent, ineffectually picking up things that might be ratchets or gaskets, suddenly said rather aggressively, 'Well, it's a matter of accuracy, isn't it, Doctor? It so happens Selby had four stings. I was in the bathroom and I saw the wasps get him. Unless you're counting the one he had a couple of days before.'

'One on his face,' Freda said, 'two on his left arm and one inside his right arm. I thought Cheryl—well, it might have taken her the same way, mightn't it?' The sob that caught her throat came out ludicrously like a hiccup. 'She's all I've got now,' she said. 'Patrick—I could have given him children. He wanted children. I'll never get married now, never, never!'

Carnaby hustled the doctor out into the hall, kicking the door shut behind him. Recalling what Bernice had said, Greenleaf wondered whether Freda's renewed cries were caused by true grief or the possible damage to the paintwork. Then, as he stood, murmuring assurances to Carnaby, the

152

penny dropped. Not the whole penny, but a fraction of it, a farthing perhaps.

'She'll be all right,' he said mechanically. 'There's nothing to worry about.' The worry was all his now.

Then he went, almost running.

Back at Shalom his deck-chair awaited him. He sat down, conscious that on his way round The Circle he had passed Sheila Macdonald and Paul Gaveston without even a smile or a wave. They had been shadows compared with the reality of his thoughts. Before his eyes he could again see Patrick's body in the bed at Hallows that Sunday morning, the thin freckled arms spread across the sheet, sleeves pushed back for coolness. And on the yellowish mottled skin red swellings. One sting on the face, two on the left arm, one on the right arm in the cubital fossa—and a fifth. There *had* been a fifth, about six inches below. Not the old sting; that had been just a scar, a purplish lump with a scab where Patrick had scratched it. The Carnabys could be wrong. Both wrong? They couldn't both be mistaken. Why should they lie? He, Greenleaf hadn't bothered to count the stings on the previous night and when he had visited Patrick in bed the blue cotton sleeves had covered both arms down to the wrists. Tamsin had been uninterested, the others embarrassed. But Carnaby had watched the wasps attack, he had been there in the line of fire, staring from the bathroom window, and Freda had sat at Patrick's feet, holding his hand. Of all the guests at the party they were in the best position to know. But at the same time he knew he wasn't wrong. *Five* stings, one on the face, two on the left arm . . .

'Hot enough for you?' It was a high-pitched irritating voice and Greenleaf didn't have to look up to know it was Nancy Gage.

'Hallo.'

'Oh, don't get up,' she said as he began to rise. 'I'll excuse

153

you. Much too hot to be polite. You men, I really pity you. Always having to bob up and down like jack-in-the-boxes.'

'I'm afraid Bernice has taken the boys into Nottingham.'

'Never mind. Actually I came to see you. Don't get me a chair. I'll sit on the grass.' She did so quite gracefully, spreading her pink cotton skirts about her like an open parasol. The renewal of love, strained and contrived though that renewal might be, was gradually restoring her beauty. It was as if she was a wilting pink and gold rose into whose leaves and stems nourishment was climbing by a slow capillarity. 'What I really came for was the name of that man who put up your summer house. We're rather spreading our wings—I don't know if Bernice told you—having an extension to our humble domain, and Mr. Glide—well, he is a bit steep, isn't he?'

'He's in the phone book Swan's the name. J. B. Swan.'

'Lovely. What a wonderful memory! What do you think? As I was coming across The Green I met that funny little Carnaby girl with an enormous lump in her lip. I asked her what it was and she said a wasp sting. She was sucking one of those filthy lollies. I ask you, the last thing! I said, now you run straight home to Mummy—I forgot she hasn't got a Mummy, just an Auntie and what an Auntie! —and get her to put bi-carbonate of soda on it.'

'Not much use, I'm afraid.'

'Oh, you doctors and your anti-biotics. I'm a great believer in the old-fashioned remedies.' She spoke with a middle-aged complacency and Greenleaf thought he knew exactly what she would be like in fifteen years' time, stout, an encyclopaedia of outworn and inaccurate advice, the very prototype of an old wife spinning old wives' tales. 'If I've said it once I've said it a dozen times, Patrick would be alive today if Tamsin had only used bi-carb.' As an after-

154

thought she exclaimed in an advertising catch phrase, 'And so reasonably priced!'

Momentarily Greenleaf closed his eyes. He opened them suddenly as she went on:

'As soon as we got back from that ghastly party I said to Oliver, you pop straight back to Hallows with some bi-carb. He hung it out a bit. Waiting for you to go, I'm afraid. Aren't we crafty? Anyway, he trotted across with his little packet . . .' It was an absurd description of the movement of that graceful, saturnine man, but Greenleaf was too interested to notice. '. . . but Tamsin must have gone to bed. She'd forgotten to lock the back door because he tried it, but that Queenie was shut up in the kitchen and she wouldn't let him in. He went round the back and all the food was still out there and Tamsin had left her presents on the birthday table, the chocolates and that bag and Crispin's flowers. She must have been terribly upset to leave it all like that. He hung about for five minutes and then he came home.'

'I expect she was tired,' Greenleaf said, his thoughts racing. So that was the answer to what he had been calling in his mind the Great White Packet Mystery. Simply Oliver Gage taking bi-carbonate of soda to his mistress's husband. And probably, he thought vulgarly, hoping for a little love on the side. No wonder he waited for me to go.

What Marvell had said about anyone being able to get into Hallows while Tamsin was out had now been shown to be manifestly false. The dog Queenie would guard her master against all comers—against all except one. The feeble motives of Edith Gaveston and Denholm Smith-King evaporated like puddles in the sun. But Tamsin had a motive, or rather many motives which crystallised into a gigantic single drive against Patrick's life. Tamsin was rich now and free. Not to marry Gage whom she had evidently sent about his business, but free to be herself in a glorious scented bright-coloured muddle.

'You're so silent,' Nancy said. 'Are you all right? I'll tell you what I'll do. I haven't got a thing on hand this afternoon. I'll nip indoors and make the poor grass widower a nice cup of tea.'

Greenleaf hated tea. He thanked her, rested his head against the canvas and closed his eyes.

14

PATRICK had died too late. Greenleaf repeated the sentence to himself as he came up to the front door of Marvell's house. Patrick had died too late. Not from the point of view of Tamsin's happiness, but medically speaking. Marvell had suggested it at the time the rumours began and Greenleaf had shrugged it off. Now he realised that it was this fact which all the time had been nagging at his mind. Had he died soon after receiving the stings or even if he had had a heart attack on seeing the picture—for Greenleaf was beginning to believe that in Patrick's history it corresponded to the something nasty in the woodshed of Freudian psychology—there would have been no mystery. But Patrick had died hours later.

Why had there been a fifth sting? A wasp in the bedroom? It was possible. Patrick had been heavily sedated. You could probably have stuck a pin in him without waking him. But why should a fifth sting kill him when four had made him only uncomfortable? He banged on the almshouse door for the second time, but Marvell wasn't at home. At last he went round to the back and sat down on the bench.

He had come for his honey and, after much heart-searching, to offer his friend a loan. Talking it over with Bernice after she came back from Nottingham, he had thought he could raise a few hundreds, enough perhaps to have the house made habitable according to the standards of Chantflower Rural Council. It was an awkward mission even though he intended to be quite pompous about it, insisting for the sake of Marvell's pride on the money being repayed at the normal rate of interest—Marvell would have to put his back into the history of Chantefleur Abbey. I am a peasant, he thought, and he is an aristocrat (the serfs to the wolves syndrome again). He might hit me. All alone in the garden, he chuckled faintly to himself. He didn't think Marvell would do that.

Presently he got up and walked about, for he was nervous. He hadn't counted on having to wait. Perhaps Marvell would be away for hours and he would have screwed up his courage in vain.

He passed the kitchen window and looking inside, saw that the table was laden with jars of honey, clear and golden, not the sugary waxen stuff you bought in the shops. There would be a pot for them and a pot for the Gages and the Gavestons. Poor though he was, Marvell was a generous man. Last year the harvest had been poor but there had been a jar on almost every Linchester table. Not Patrick's though. Patrick recoiled from honey as if it were poison.

Greenleaf turned away and began to follow the path towards the orchard. Under the trees he stopped and sat down on the stump of a withered ancient apple Marvell had felled in the winter. Apple, plum and pear leaves made a dappled pattern on the turf as the sunlight filtered through gnarled branches. All about him he could hear the muted yet ominous hum of the bees that had been robbed of their treasure. Marvell, he guessed, had reimbursed them, giving them—as he put it—silver for their gold. He had once shown the doctor the tacky grey candy he made for them from boiled sugar. But, just the same, bewilderment over their loss made them angry.

There were three hives made of white painted wood and

this had surprised Greenleaf the first time he had seen them for he had expected the igloos of plaited straw you see in children's picture books. Beneath the entrance to each hive— a slit between the two lowest boards—was a wooden step or platform on to which the bees issued, trickling forth in a thin dark stream. There was a suggestion of liquid in their movement, measured yet turbulent, regular and purposeful. Marvell had told him something of their ordered social life, and because of this rather than from the interest of a naturalist, he approached the hive and knelt down before it.

At first the bees ignored him. He put his ear to the wall of the hive and listened. From inside there came the sound as of a busy city where thousand upon thousand of workers feed, love, breed and engage in industry. He could hear a soft roar, constant in volume, changing in pitch. There was warmth in it and richness and an immense controlled activity.

For a moment he had forgotten that these insects were not simply harvesters; they were armed. Then, as he eased himself into a sitting position, one of them appeared suddenly from a tree or perhaps from the roof of the hive. It skimmed his hair and sank on the windless air until it was in front of his eyes. He got up hastily and brushed at it and at the others which began to gather about it. How horrible, how treacherous Nature could be! You contemplated it with the eye of an aesthete or a sociologist, and just as you were beginning to see there might be something in it after all, it rose and struck you, attacked you . . . He gasped and ran, glad that there was no-one to see him. Two of the bees followed him, sailing on the hot fruit-scented air. He stripped off his jacket and flung it over his head. Panting with panic and with sudden revelation, he stumbled into Marvell's garden shed.

The bee-keeper's veiled hat and calico coat were suspended from the roof, taped gloves protruding from the sleeves. The clothes looked like a guy or a hanged man. When he had slammed the door between himself and his pursuers, he sat down on the garden roller, sweating. He knew now how Patrick Selby had died.

'But wouldn't he have swelled up?' Bernice asked. 'I thought the histamine made you swell up all over.'

'Yes, it does.' Greenleaf bent over the kitchen sink, washing tool-shed cobwebs from his hands. 'I gave him antihistamine . . .'

'Why didn't it work, Max?'

'I expect it did, up to a point. Don't forget, Patrick wasn't allergic to wasp stings. But if he was allergic to *bee* stings, as I think he must have been, the histamine reaction would have been very strong. Two hundred milligrammes of antihistamine wouldn't have gone anywhere. The only thing for people with that sort of allergy is an injection of adrenalin given as soon as possible. If they don't have it they die very quickly.' She shivered and he went on: 'Patrick didn't have that injection. He was heavily sedated, he couldn't call for help and if there was no-one near . . .' He shrugged. 'There would have been a lot of swelling but the swelling would gradually disappear. I didn't see him till ten or eleven hours after he died. His face was a bit puffy and I put it down to the wasp sting under the eye. By the time Glover got to work on him—well! '

'An accident?'

'To much of a coincidence. Four wasp stings and then you get stung by a bee in your own bedroom?'

'He must have known he was allergic to bee stings.'

'Not necessarily, although I think he did. He hated honey. Remember? He knew about it all right and someone else knew too.'

'You mean he told someone?'

'Bernice, I have to say this. At the moment I can only say it to you, but I may have to tell the police. People with this sort of allergy usually find out about it when they're children. They get stung, have the adrenalin, and afterwards they're careful never to get another. But others know about it, the people who were there at the time.' Turning his back on the window behind which Nature seemed to seethe, he looked at the manufactured, man-made things in the modern kitchen, and at civilised, corseted, powdered Bernice. 'Tamsin and Patrick weren't only husband and wife; they were cousins. They'd known each other since they were children. Even if he half-forgot it, never spoke of it, she might remember.

'So simple, wasn't it? Patrick has the wasp stings and he takes the sodium amytal to make him sleep heavily. When he's asleep she goes to the only place where she can be sure of getting hold of a bee, Marvell's orchard, and she takes with her a *straw* handbag.'

'I see. Straw for ventilation, you mean. The bee wouldn't suffocate. She found the bee before Crispin saw her. But why stay there, why make love to him?'

'I don't know. So it was a good excuse for coming? I tell you I don't know, Bernice. But when she got back Patrick was under heavy sedation. You could have stuck a pin in him.'

'Oh, Max, don't!'

'I'm going over to see her now.' He brushed away the warning hand Bernice rested on his arm. 'I have to,' he said.

She was loading cases into the big car, Patrick's car, when he came slowly between the silver-green crinolines of the willows. The car was standing in front of the double doors and Queenie was lying on the driving seat watching the flights of swifts that swooped across the garden, off-course from their hunting ground on The Green.

'I'm leaving tomorrow, Max,' she said. He took the biggest case from her and lifted it into the boot. 'Such a mad rush! I've sold my house and the solicitor's dealing with everything. Queenie and I—we don't know where we're going but we're going to drive and drive. All the furniture—they've bought that too. I shan't have anything but my clothes and the car—I've sold the Mini—and oh, Max! I shall have enough money to live on for the rest of my life.'

The mask had not slipped at all. Only her lips, russet against the egg-shell brown of her face, smiled and swelled the lineless cheeks.

'Leave Queenie,' she said, for Greenleaf, no lover of animals, was caressing the dog's neck to hide his embarrassment and his fear. 'She thinks she's a bird dog. Come into the house.'

He followed her into the dining-room. The picture had been taken down and was resting against the wall. Was she planning to take it with her or have it sent on? She must have seen him hesitate for she took his hand and drew him to a chair by the window. He sat down with his back to the painted thing.

'You don't like it, do you?'

Greenleaf, unable to smile, wrinkled his nose.

'Not much.'

'Patrick didn't like it either.' Her voice sounded like a little girl's, puzzled, naive. 'Really, too silly! He wasn't awfully mature, you know. I mean, people grow out of things like that, don't they? Like being frightened of the dark.'

'Not always.' In a moment he would have to begin questioning her. He had no idea how she would react. In films, in plays, they confessed and either grew violent or threw themselves upon your mercy. His mission nauseated him.

She went on dreamily, apparently suspecting nothing:

'That picture, it used to hang in a room in my grandmother's house in London. The garden room we called it because it opened into a sort of conservatory. Patrick made an awful fuss the first time he saw it—well, the only time really. My uncle and aunt had come home from America and they stayed a couple of nights with my grandmother. Patrick was terribly spoilt.' She swivelled round until her eyes seemed to meet the eyes of Salome. 'He was nine and I was seven. Grandmother thought he was wonderful.' Her laughter was dry and faintly bitter. 'She never had to live with him. But she was fair, my grandmother, fair at the end. She left her money to me. So sweet!'

If only she would tell him something significant, something to make him feel justified in setting in motion the machinery that would send this sprite-like creature, this breathless waif of a woman, to a long incarceration. And yet . . . Tamsin in Holloway, Tamsin coarsened, roughened in speech and in manners. It was unthinkable.

'That was nice for you,' he said stupidly.

'I loved her, you know, but she was a bit mad. Patrick's father committing suicide, it sent her over the edge. It gave her a sort of pathological fear of divorce.'

This is it, he thought. He needed to hear and at the same time he wanted to stop her. Almost unconsciously he fumbled along the window sill.

'Did you want a cigarette, Max?'

Taking one from the silver box, he said, 'I've given it up,' and lit it with shaking fingers.

'What was I saying? Oh, yes, about Grandmother. She knew I wasn't getting on all that well with Patrick. Funny, she made the match and she wanted us to make a go of it. Just because we were cousins she thought we'd be alike. How wrong she was! After she died we went along to hear the will read—like they do in books. Dramatic, I can't tell you! Patrick wasn't mentioned at all. I don't know if she thought he'd had enough from his father—that went on this house—or perhaps she resented it because he never went to see her. Anyway, she left all her money to me, the income, not the capital, on condition . . .'

She paused as the dog padded in and Greenleaf listened, cursing the diversion.

'On condition Patrick and I were never divorced!'

O God, he thought, how it all fits, a pattern, a puzzle like those things the boys used to have, when you have to make the ball bearings drop into the right slots.

'As if I wanted to be divorced,' she said. 'I can't support myself. They were too busy educating him to bother about me.'

But Patrick had been going to divorce her. She would have had nothing. Without money from her Oliver Gage would have been unable to marry her, for the costs of her divorce and Nancy's would have fallen on him. Like everyone else he must have been deceived about her income until she got cold feet and told him. He pictured her confessing to Gage; then, when he recoiled from her, running ashamed and wretched—for Tamsin, he was sure, was no nympho-maniac—to Marvell, her last resort. When Marvell refused her there was only one way out . . .

'Does anybody know?' he asked sharply, not bothering to conceal a curiosity she must take for impertinence.

'It was so humiliating,' she said, whispering now. 'Every-body thought I was quite well-off, independent. But if Patrick had divorced me I would have been—I would have been destitute.'

164

It was a sudden bare revelation of motive and it recalled him to the real business of his visit.

'Tamsin . . .' he began. The cigarette was making him feel a little dizzy, and to his eyes, focussing badly, the woman in the chair opposite was just a blur of brown and bright green. 'I came to tell you something very serious. About Patrick . . .'

'You mean Freda Carnaby? I know all about that. Please! They were the same kind of people, Max. They really suited each other. If Patrick could have made anyone happy it was Freda Carnaby. But you mustn't think I drove him to it. It was only because of that—Oliver and me . . . I was so lonely, Max.'

He was horrified that she should think him capable of repeating gossip to her and to stop her he blundered into the middle of it, forgetting his doctor's discretion.

'No, no. I meant Patrick's death. I don't think he died of heart failure.'

Was it possible that, immured here since her return, she had heard nothing of the gossip? She turned on him, quivering and he wondered if this was the beginning of the violence he expected.

'He must have,' she cried. 'Max, this isn't something that'll stop me going tomorrow, is it? He was so hateful to me when he was alive and now he's dead—I can feel him still in the house.'

So intense was her tone that Greenleaf half-turned towards the door.

'You see what I mean? Sometimes when I go upstairs I think to myself, suppose I see his writing in the dust on the dressing-table? That's what he used to do. I'm not much of a housewife, Max, and we couldn't keep a woman. They were all frightened of Queenie. When I hadn't cleaned

165

properly he used to write in the dust "Dust this" or "I do my job, you do yours". He *did*.'

Were some marriages really like that? Yes, it fitted with what he had known of Patrick's character. He could imagine a freckled finger with a close-trimmed nail moving deliberately across the black glass, crossing the t, dotting the i.

Although he knew her moods, how suddenly hysteria was liable to wistfulness or vague reminiscing, he was startled when she burst out in a ragged voice:

'I'm afraid to go in his room! He's dead but suppose—suppose the writing was there just the same?'

'Tamsin.' He must put an end to this. 'How many wasp stings did Patrick have?'

She was still tense, hunched in her chair, frightened of the dead man and the house he had built.

'Four. Does it matter? You said he didn't die of the stings.' The air in the room was pleasantly warm but she got up and closed the door. It was stupid to feel uneasy, to remember the frightened charwoman, the Smith-King children. She sat down again and he reflected that they were shut in now with the strong watchful dog and that all the neighbours were away on holiday.

'How many did he have when he came in from the garden?'

'Well, four. I told you. I didn't look.'

'And after—when he was dead?'

He stubbed out the cigarette and held his hands tightly together in his lap. His eyes were on her as she coaxed the Weimaraner to her chair, softly snapping her fingers and finally closing them over the pearled fawn snout.

'There, my Queenie, my beauty . . .' Dry brown cheek pressed against wet brown nose, two pairs of eyes looking at him.

'I think he was stung by a bee, Tamsin.'

At a word from her the dog would spring. For armour

he had only the long curtains that hung against the window blinds. Wrapped around him they would protect him for a moment, but the dog's teeth would rip that velvet and then . . . ?

'Stung by a *bee*?'

'Perhaps it was an accident. A bee could have got into the bedroom—'

'Oh, no.' She spoke firmly and decisively for her. 'It couldn't happen that way.' Her mouth was close to the dog's ear now. She whispered something, loosening her fingers from Queenie's dewlap. Greenleaf felt something knock within his chest like a hand beating suddenly against his ribs. But it was ridiculous, absurd, such things couldn't happen! The dog broke free. He braced himself, forgetting convention, pride, the courage a man is supposed to show, and covered his face as the chair skidded back across the polished floor.

15

F O R one of those seconds that take an age to live through
he was caught up in fear and fettered to the chair. His eyes
closed, he waited for the hot breath and the trickling saliva.
Tamsin's voice came sweet and anticlimactic.

'Oh, Max, I'm awfully sorry. That floor! The furniture's
always sliding about.'

I make a bad policeman, he thought, blinking and adjust-
ing his chair back in its position by the window. But where
was the dog and why wasn't he in the process of being
mauled? Then he saw her, puffing and blowing under the
sideboard in pursuit of—an earwig!

'You baby, Queenie. She'll hunt anything, even insects.'
It was all right. The drama had been nothing but a domestic
game with a pet. And Tamsin, he saw, had noticed only that
he was startled by the sudden skidding of a chair. 'Talking
of insects,' she said, 'it's funny about the bee. It's a coincidence, in a way. You see, that's what happened when Patrick
first saw the picture. I'd never seen him before and I was
watching from the garden. He ran into the conservatory and
there was a bee on a geranium. He put out his hand and it
stung him.'

The shock was subsiding now.

'What happened?' he asked rather shakily.

Tamsin shrugged and pulled Queenie out by the tail.

'Why, nothing happened. It made me laugh. Children are

168

cruel, aren't they? Grandmother and my aunt, they made a dreadful fuss. They put him to bed and the doctor came. I remember I said, "He must be an awful coward to have the doctor for a bee sting. I bet you wouldn't have got the doctor for me," and they sent me to my room. I told him about it when we were older but he wouldn't talk about it. He only said he didn't like bees and he couldn't stand honey.'

'Didn't it ever occur to you that he might be allergic to bee stings?'

'I didn't know you could be,' she said, her eyes wide with surprise.

He almost believed her. He wanted to believe her, to say, 'Yes, you can go. Be happy, Tamsin. Drive and drive—far away!'

Now more than ever it seemed likely that the bee had got there by chance. Hadn't he opened the window in the balcony room himself? Wasps stung when they were provoked; perhaps the same was true of bees and Patrick's killer, alighting on his exposed arm, had been alerted into venom by a twitch or a galvanic start from the sleeping man. If Tamsin were guilty she would clutch at the possibility of an accident and no law could touch her.

'I asked you about an accident,' he said. 'Could a bee have stung him by accident?'

'I suppose so.' Marvell is wrong, he thought. She isn't clever. She's stupid, sweetly stupid and vague. She lives a life of her own, a life of dreams sustained by unearned, unquestioned money. But dreams can change into nightmares . . .

Then she said something that entirely altered the picture he had made of her. She was not stupid, nor was she a murderess.

'Oh, but it couldn't!' Dreamy, vague children often do best in examinations, drawing solutions from their inner lives. 'I know it couldn't. Crispin told me something about bees once. They're different from wasps and when they sting they die. It's like a sort of hara-kiri, Max. They leave the sting behind and a bit of their own inside with it. Don't you think it's horrid for them, poor bees? The sting would still have been in Patrick's arm if it had been an accident. We'd have seen it!'

Unwittingly he had given her a loophole. A guilty woman would have wriggled through it. Tamsin, in her innocence, was confirming that her husband had been murdered.

'Max, you don't mean you think I . . . ?

'No, Tamsin, no.'

'I'm glad he's dead. I am. I tried everything I could to make him forgive me over Oliver and give that woman up. But he wouldn't. He said I'd given him the chance he'd been waiting for. Now he could divorce me and Freda's name wouldn't have to be brought into it at all. Oh, outwardly he was perfectly friendly to Oliver, but all the time he was having his flat in town watched. Oliver and Nancy must come to the party. Then, when he'd got everything lined up he was going to drop his bombshell.' She paused and drew a little sobbing breath, rubbing away the frown lines with her ringless fingers. 'He liked to make people suffer, Max. Even the Smith-Kings. Did you see how he was torturing Denholm at the party?' When Greenleaf said nothing she went on in a shaky voice that fell sometimes to a whisper, 'Oh, that awful party! The evening before, he went straight to Freda's house. I was desperate, I cried and cried for hours. Oliver came but I wouldn't let him in. All those weeks when we were at the flat he'd been hinting that he'd get Nancy to divorce him. My money would pay for that and keep us both. I had to tell him there wouldn't be any money. I did tell him at last, Max, I told him at the party.'

And Gage had sat beside her gloomily, Greenleaf remembered. There had been no close sensual dancing after that.

'He went on and on about it. He even tried to think of ways of upsetting the will. But d'you know something? I don't want to be married. I've had enough of marriage.' Her voice grew harsh and strident. 'But I'd have married anyone who would have supported me. Can you see me working in an office, Max, going home to a furnished room and cooking things on a gas ring? I'd even have married Crispin!'

'Marvell hasn't any money,' he said. 'His house is falling down and he won't get much for the land.'

She was thunderstruck. The mask slipped at last and her big golden eyes widened and blazed.

'But his books . . . ?'

'I don't believe he ever finishes them.'

To him it was the saddest of stories, that Marvell should have to leave the house he loved, that her nightmare of the room with the gas ring might become real to him. Because of this her ringing laughter was an affront. Peal upon peal of it rang through the room; hot laughter to burn and cleanse away all her old griefs. The Weimaraner squatted, alert, startled.

'What's so funny?'

She no longer cared what he might think or say.

'It's mad, it's ridiculous! He spent the night here, you know, the night Patrick died. He spent it with me. I was so scared when you made me sit on the bed in the back bedroom. I felt you must sense that—that I hadn't been alone. Oh, Max, Max, don't you see how crazy it is?' He stared, his hurt suspicion melting, for he saw that she was laughing at herself. 'I wanted to marry him for his money,' she said, 'and he wanted to marry me for mine, and the mad thing is we hadn't either of us got a bean!'

16

SHE walked with him to the gate. He shook hands with her and impulsively—because he was ashamed of the thoughts he had harboured—kissed her cheek.

'Can I go tomorrow? Will it be all right, Max?' She spoke to him as if he *were* a policeman or a Home Office official. In denying the possibility of accidental death she had declared, if not in words, that Patrick had been murdered. But Greenleaf knew she hadn't realised it yet. Sometime it would reach her, surfacing on to her mind through that rich, jumbled subconscious, and then perhaps it would register no more strongly than the memory of a sharp word or an unfriendly face. By then she might be driving away on the road that led—where? To another terse young company director who would be fascinated for a time by witchlike innocence? Greenleaf wondered as he drew his lips from her powderless cheek.

'Good-bye, Tamsin,' he said.

When he came to the Linchester Manor gates he looked back and waved. She stood in the twilight, one hand upraised, the other on the dog's neck. Then she turned, moving behind the willows, and he saw her no more.

He entered Marvell's garden by way of the orchard gate. The bees were still active and he gave the hives a wide berth.

It occurred to him that Marvell might still be out but if this were so he would wait—if necessary all night.

By now it was growing dark. A bat brushed his face and wheeled away. For a second he saw it silhouetted against the jade-coloured sky like a tiny pterodactyl. He came to the closed lattice and looked in. No lamps were lit but the china still showed dim gleams from the last of the light. At first he thought the room must be empty. The stillness about the whole place was uncanny. Nothing moved. Then he saw between the wing and the arm of a chair that had its back to the window a sliver of white sleeve and he knew Marvell must be sitting there.

He knocked at the back door. No footsteps, no sound of creaking or the movement of castors across the floor. The door wasn't locked. He unlatched it, passed the honey-laden table and walked into the living room. Marvell wasn't asleep. He lay back in his chair, his hands folded loosely in his lap, staring at the opposite wall. In the grate—the absurd pretty grate that shone like black silver—was a pile of charred paper. Greenleaf knew without having to ask that Marvell had been burning his manuscript.

'I came earlier,' he said. 'I had something to ask you. It doesn't matter now.'

Marvell smiled, stretched and sat up.

'I went to tell Glide he could have the land,' he said. 'You can take your honey, if you like. It's ready.'

Greenleaf would never eat honey again as long as he lived. He began to feel sick, but not afraid, not at all afraid. His eyes met Marvell's and because he couldn't bear to look into the light blue ones, steady, mocking, unfathomably sad, he took off his glasses and began polishing them against his lapel.

'You know, don't you? Yes, I see that you know.'

173

Hazily, myopically, Greenleaf felt for the chair and sat down on the edge of it. The wooden arms felt cold.

'Why?' he asked. His voice sounded terribly loud until he realised that they had been speaking in whispers. 'Why, Crispin?' And the Christian name, so long withheld, came naturally.

'Money? Yes, of course, money. It's the only real temptation, Max. Love, beauty, power, they are the obverse side of the coin that is money.'

From his dark corner Greenleaf said: 'She wouldn't have had any if Patrick had divorced her. That was the condition in the will.' The man's surprise was real but, unlike Tamsin, he didn't laugh. 'You didn't know?'

'No, I didn't know.'

'Then . . . ?'

'I wanted more. Can't you see, Max? That place, that glass palace. . . . With the money from that and his money and her money, what couldn't I have done here?' He spread his arms wide as if he would take the whole room, the whole house into his embrace. 'Tell me—I'm curious to know— what did she want from me?'

'Money.'

He sighed.

'I thought I would know love,' he said. 'But, of course, I do see. That kind of sale is a woman's privilege. May I tell you about it?'

Greenleaf nodded.

'Shall we have some light?'

'I'd rather not,' the doctor said.

'Yes, I suppose you would feel that way. I think that like Alice I had better begin at the beginning, go on till I get to the end, and then stop.'

What sort of a man was this that could talk of children's books on the edge of the abyss?

'As you like.'

'When Glide told me about the house I thought I had come to the end of my world. The bright day is done and we are for the dark.' He paused for a moment and rubbed his eyes. 'Max, I told you the truth and nothing but the truth, but I didn't tell you the whole truth. You know that?'

'You told me one lie.'

'Just one. We'll leave that for the moment. I said I'd begin at the beginning but I don't know where the beginning was. Perhaps it was last year when Tamsin was helping me extract the honey. She said Patrick didn't like it. He was afraid of bees and everything associated with them, but he'd only been stung once. That was when he was a little boy at their grandmother's house. He'd been frightened by a picture of a girl holding a man's head on a plate and he'd run into the conservatory. A bee stung him on his hand.'

'Yes, she told me.'

'Max, she didn't know why the doctor had been sent for. She thought it was because Patrick was a spoiled brat. She didn't know why the doctor had given him an injection, had stayed for hours. But at the time I was reading a book about allergies. I was interested because of that damned hay fever. When she'd gone I looked up bee stings and I found why the doctor had stayed and what kind of an injection Patrick had had. He must have been allergic to bee stings. I didn't say anything to Tamsin. I don't know why not. Perhaps, even then . . . I don't know, Max.'

'Some people grow up out of allergies,' Greenleaf said.

'I know that too. But if it didn't come off, who would know?'

'It did come off.'

Marvell went on as if he hadn't spoken.

'It wasn't premeditated. Or, if it was, the meditation only

175

took a few minutes. It began with the picture. I don't know this part—I'm only guessing—but I think that when Tamsin was offered the picture things were all right between her and Patrick, as right as they ever were. Of course she knew he'd hated it when he was a child but she thought he'd grown out of that.'

'When it arrived,' Greenleaf said slowly, 'she must have been trying to patch things up between them. He might think she'd sent for it to annoy him, so she had it put in her room, a room he never went into.'

'I saw it—and, Max, I told them about it in all innocence! '

'Tamsin was past caring then.'

He must be kind, not a policeman, not an inquisitor.

'Go on,' he said gently.

'It was only when Patrick reacted the way he did that I remembered the bee sting. The temptation, Max! I was sick with temptation. I don't know how I got down those stairs.'

'I remember,' Greenleaf said. 'I remember what you said. Something about the eye of childhood fearing a painted devil. I thought it was just another quotation.'

Marvell smiled a tight bitter smile.

'It is. Macbeth. It doesn't mean that in the text. It doesn't mean that Macbeth was looking with a child's memory, but only in a childish way. I suppose it was my subconscious that gave it that meaning. I knew that Patrick feared it because of what had happened when he *was* a child. Then the wasps got him. Even then I couldn't see my opportunity. I wasn't sure of Tamsin. I'd never made love to her. For all I knew I was just an old pedagogue to her, a domestic science teacher. At midnight she came into my orchard.'

'But she wasn't carrying that straw bag,' Greenleaf said quickly. 'It wasn't at all her style. Besides, when Oliver Gage came round with the bi-carb Tamsin was out but the bag was on the birthday table.'

176

Marvell got up and, crossing to the window, opened the casement. 'My one lie,' he said. Greenleaf watched him drawing in great breaths of the dark blue air. 'Will you be in a draught?'

'It doesn't matter.'

'I felt—I felt suddenly as if I was going to faint.' From shock? From fear? Greenleaf wondered with dismay if for months now Marvell hadn't been getting enough to eat. 'I'll close it now.' He shifted with precise fingers the long wisps of Tradescantia. 'I'd like the lamp. You don't mind?' When Greenleaf shook his head, he said urgently, 'Darkness—darkness is a kind of poverty.'

When the lamp was lit Marvell put his hands round it. They had the opacity age brings and the thought came to Greenleaf that had his son's hands covered that incandescence the light would have seeped through them as through red panes.

'It all happened as I've told you,' Marvell went on, 'except that I didn't say no to Tamsin. I told her I'd walk back with her but that I'd left my jacket in the orchard. I went down to the shed to get my gloves and my veil and a little box with a mesh lid. Someone had once sent it to me with a queen bee in it.

'When we got to Hallows I went in with her. She'd told me you'd given Patrick a sedative and we both knew I was going to stay with her. We didn't say it but we knew. She didn't want to look at Patrick and she went to take a shower. While she was in the bathroom and I could hear the water running I went into Patrick's room. I still wasn't sure the sting wouldn't wake him. There was a big pincushion on the dressing-table. I took a pin and stuck it very lightly into him. He didn't stir.'

Greenleaf felt a deathly cold creep upon him, a chill that culminated in a tremendous galvanic shudder.

'Then I put the bee on his arm and I—I teased it, Max, till it stung him.' He slid his hands down the lamp until they lay flat and fan-spread on the table. 'I can't tell you how I hated doing it. I know it's sentimental, but the bees were my friends. They'd worked for me faithfully and every year I took their honey away from them, all their treasure. They'd fed me—sometimes I didn't have anything but bread and honey to eat for days on end. Now I was forcing one of them to kill itself for my sake. It plunged its sting into those disgusting freckles. . . . My God, Max, it was horrible to see it trying to fly and then keeling over. Horrible!'

Greenleaf started to speak. He checked himself and crouched in his chair. They were not on the same wavelength, a country G.P. and this naturalist who could kill a man and mourn the death of an insect.

Marvell smiled grimly. 'I had to stay after that. I had to stay and see she didn't go into that room. She hated Patrick but I don't think she would have stood by and let him die.' He stood up straight and in the half-dark he was young again. 'I made love to Tamsin under the eyes of Herod's niece.' His shoulders bowed as if to receive age like a cloak. 'At the time I thought it a pretty conceit. I should have remembered, Max, that they might both understand the desires of old men. I thought it was love.'

He sat on the table edge and swung his legs.

'I left at four. She was asleep and Patrick was dead. I checked. The dog came upstairs and I shut her in with Tamsin.

'Perhaps I was vain, Max, perhaps I thought I had a kind of *droit de seigneur*, perhaps I'm just old-fashioned. You see, I thought that still meant something to a woman, that she would have to marry me. When she made it plain she didn't want me, I felt—My God! She'd wanted me before, but I'm fifty and she's twenty-seven. I thought . . .'

'Crispin, I *do* see.' It was more horrible than Greenleaf had thought it could be. He hadn't anticipated this grubbing into the roots of another man's manhood. Please don't. I never wanted to. . . .'

'But it was only money, always money.' He laughed harshly but quite sanely into Greenleaf's face. 'It's all better now, all better. I am Antony still!'

'But why?' Greenleaf asked again. 'Why tell me so much?' He felt angry, but his anger was a tiny spark in the fire of his other emotions: amazement, pity and a kind of grief. 'You led me into this. You made me suspect.' He spread his hands, then gripped the chair arms.

Marvell said calmly: 'Naturally, I intended to get away with it at first.' His face was a gentle blank. He might have been describing to the doctor his methods of pruning a fruit tree. 'But when I knew that I had killed Patrick in vain, for nothing, I wanted—I suppose I wanted to salvage something from the waste. They say criminals are vain.' With a kind of wonder he said: 'I *am* a criminal. My God, I hadn't thought of it like that before. I don't think it was that sort of vanity. All the moves in the game, they seemed like a puzzle. I thought a doctor and only a doctor could solve it. That's why I picked on you, Max.'

He made a little half-sketched movement towards Greenleaf as if he was going to touch him. Then he withdrew his hand.

'I meant to try to get you interested. Then Nancy started it all off for me. I've always thought hatred was such an uncivilised thing, but I really hated Tamsin. When you suspected her I thought, to hell with Tamsin!' He raised his eyebrows and he smiled. 'If it had come to it, perhaps. . . . I don't think I could have let her suffer for what I did.'

179

'Didn't you think what it would mean if I found out?'

Marvell moved to the fireplace and taking a match from the box on the mantelpiece struck it and dropped it among the charred sheets of the manuscript. A single spiring flame rose and illuminated his face.

'Mac,' he said, 'I had nothing to hope for. I've had a fine life, a good life. You know, I've always thought that was the true end of man, tilling the soil, husbanding the fruits of the soil, making wonderful things from a jar of honey, a basket of rose petals. In the evenings I wrote about the things of the past, I talked to people who remembered like me the days before taxes and death duties took away almost everything that made life for people like me a kind of—a kind of golden dream. Oh, I know it was a dream. I wasn't a particularly useful member of society but I wasn't a drag on society either. Just a drone watching the workers and waiting for the summer to end. My summer ended when Glide told me about this house. That's what I meant when I said the bright day was done and I was for the dark.' As the flame died he turned from the fireplace and clasping his hands behind his back looked down at Greenleaf.

'I don't know what to do,' the doctor said. It was the phrase of despair, the sentence desperate people used to him from the other side of the consulting room table.

Marvell said practically: 'There's only one thing you can do, isn't there? You can't be a party to a felony. You're not a priest hearing confession.'

'I wish,' Greenleaf said, a world of bitterness making his voice uneven, 'I wish I'd kept to it when I said I didn't want to hear.'

'I should have made you.'

'For God's sake!' He jumped up and they faced each other in the circle of yellow light. 'Stop playing God with me!'

'Max, it's all over. I'll have a wash, I'll put some things in a bag. Then we'll go to the police together.' As the doctor's face clouded he said quickly. 'You can stay with me if you like.'

'I'll wait for you.' Not here though. In the garden. 'I'm not a policeman.' How many times had he said that in the past weeks? Or had he in fact said it only to himself in a repetitive refrain that irritated his days and curled itself around his sleep?

Marvell hesitated. Something leaped into his eyes but all he said was: 'Max . . . forgive me?' Then when the doctor said nothing he picked up the lamp and carried it before him into the passage.

The garden was a paradise of sweet scents. At first Greenleaf was too bemused, too stunned for thought. He moved across the grass watching his own shadow going before him, black on the silvered grass. The great trees shivered and an owl flying high crossed the dappled face of the moon.

In the house behind him he could see the lamplight through a single window, the bathroom window. The rest of Marvell's home was as dark and as still as if Glide had already bought it, as if it was waiting with a kind of squat resignation the coming of the men with the bulldozers. A year would elapse perhaps, only six months if the weather held. Then another house would arise, the mock-Tudor phoenix of some Nottingham business man, on the ashes of the cottages Andreas Quercus had made when George I held court in London.

The light was still on. No shadow moved across it. I must leave him in peace, Greenleaf thought, for a few more minutes. He has lived alone, loving loneliness, and he may never be alone again.

Avoiding the orchard where the bees were, he walked in

a circle around the lawn until he came once more to the back door. He went in slowly, feeling his way in the dark. His fingers touched the uneven walls, crept across the plates, the framed lithographs. At the bathroom door he stopped and listened. No sound came. Suddenly as he stood, looking down at the strip of light between door and floor, he thought of another house, another bathroom where Tamsin had showered her slim brown body while her lover gave to Patrick the sting that was his own individual brand of death.

He paced the narrow passage, sickness churning his belly and rising into his throat. When he could stand it no more he called, 'Crispin!' The silence was driving him into a panic. 'Crispin, Crispin!' He banged on the heavy old door with hands so numb and nerveless that they seemed no part of his tense body.

In a film or a play he would have put his shoulder to that door and it would have yielded like cardboard, but he knew without trying how impossible it was for him to attempt to shift this two-inch thick chunk of oak. Instead he groped his way back, wondering what that noise was that pumped and throbbed in the darkness. When he reached the open air he realised that it was the beating of his own heart.

He had to make himself look through that lighted window, pulling his hands from his eyes as a man pulls back curtains on to an unwelcome day. The glass was old and twisted, the light poor but good enough to show him what he was afraid to see.

The bath was full of blood.

No, it couldn't be—not all blood. There must be water, gallons of water, but it looked like blood, thin, scarlet and immobile. Marvell's face rested above the water line—the blood line—and the withdrawing of life had also withdrawn age and the lines of age. So had the head looked in Salome's silver platter.

Greenleaf heard someone sob. He almost looked round. Then he knew that it was he who had sobbed. He took off his jacket, struggling with it as a man struggles with clothes in a dream, and wrapped it around his fist and his arm. The window broke noisily. Greenleaf unlatched the casement and squeezed in over the sill.

Marvell was dead but warm and limp. He lifted the slack arms and saw first the slashes on the wrists, then the cut-throat razor lying beneath the translucent red water. Greenleaf knew no history but there came to him as he held the dead hands the memory of a lecture by the professor of Forensic Medicine. The Romans, he had said, took death in this way, letting out life into warm water. What had Marvell said? 'I am Antony still' and 'Max, forgive me.'

Greenleaf touched nothing more although he would have liked to drain the bath and cover the body. He unlocked the door, carrying the lamp with him, and left Marvell in the darkness he had chosen.

Half-way across the living room he stopped and on an impulse unhooked from the wall the olive-coloured plate with the twig and the apple. As it slid into his pocket he felt with fingers that had palpated human scars the bruise on the underside of the glazed fruit.

The wood with its insinuating branches was not for him tonight. He blew out the lamp and went home by Long Lane.

On Linchester the houses were still lit, the Gages' noisy with gramophone music, the Gavestons' glowing, its windows crossed and re-crossed by moving shadows. As he came to Shalom a taxi passed him, women waved, and Walter Miller's face, brown as a conker, grinned at him from under a pink straw hat. Home to Linchester, home to autumn, home to the biggest sensation they had ever known. . . .

Bernice opened the door before he could get his key out.

'Darling, you're ill! What's happened?' she cried and she put her arms round him, holding him close.

'Give me a kiss,' he said, and when she had done so he lifted her arms from his neck and placed them gently at her sides. 'I'll tell you about it,' he said, 'but not now. Now I have to telephone.'

A DEMON IN MY VIEW

Ruth Rendell

In a gloomy cellar the figure of a woman leans against the wall. Palely beautiful, she makes no move when the man advances on her from the shadows, puts his hands around her neck and strangles her.

Arthur Johnson is prim, fifty and a bachelor. To the outside world he is the very picture of respectability. No one knows of the dark lusts that bind Arthur to the pale lady in the cellar.

Then, one day, the lady is gone and a new victim must be found . . .

'Absolutely unputdownable . . . it is stamped on every page with the firm mark of a distinguished storyteller at the very height of her powers' *Graham Lord, Sunday Express*

FROM DOON WITH DEATH

Ruth Rendell

'Britain's leading lady crime novelist' *Sunday Express*

Margaret Parsons and her husband had just moved back to the small village in which she had grown up. They lived an uneventful, anonymous life and had nothing to hide.

Why then is Margaret found horribly strangled in a wood? Why do her childhood friends deny even having known her? And who is the secret admirer who has been sending her books of poetry?

SOME LIE AND SOME DIE

Ruth Rendell

For a while the pop festival at 'Sundays' went well. The sun shone, the groups played and everyone – except a few angry neighbours – seemed to enjoy themselves.

Then the weather changed. And in a nearby quarry two lovers found a body that made even Inspector Wexford's stomach lurch.

Dawn Stonor had been a local girl – back from London on a flying visit that not even her mother could explain – and the only clue that Wexford had was her strange connection with the star of the festival . . .

'One of the best crime novelists writing today' *Sunday Express*

NO MORE DYING THEN

Ruth Rendell

The mysterious death of little Stella Rivers was still fresh in the minds of everyone who lived in Kingsmarkham. No one wanted a repetition of that harrowing time. So when a five-year-old boy vanished the whole police force moved feverishly into action.

Chief Inspector Wexford thinks he knows all the obvious places to search . . . and whom to suspect. But there are no clues whatsoever – none, that is, until the anonymous letters start arriving . . .

MURDER BEING ONCE DONE

Ruth Rendell

'DEATH ONLY IS REAL'
So read the grim epitaph on a family vault. Appropriate
enough, for it was here, amid the decay and desolation of
Kenbourne Vale Cemetery, that the girl's body was found.

Detective Chief Inspector Wexford was in London for a rest
but he soon found himself deeply involved in this baffling
case.

A SLEEPING LIFE

Ruth Rendell

Kingsmarkham was one of those close-knit communities where everyone knew everyone else's business; so when Rhoda Comfrey's body was found under a hedge, Chief Inspector Wexford felt sure the case would be a simple one.

But although the victim was a familiar face to the locals, there was absolutely no evidence that she existed – no address book, no driving licence – nothing but forty-two pounds and three keys. But when Wexford begins to tackle the case, it turns into a maddening labyrinth of blind alleys.

A JUDGEMENT IN STONE

Ruth Rendell

Eunice Parchman applied for the job of housekeeper to the Coverdale family on the same kind of impulse that made her buy a box of chocolates or smother her invalid father. *If* they had been less desperate for help in their country house, they might never have employed her. *If* they had treated her less kindly, she might never have hated them. *If* they had never discovered her terrible secret, she might not have murdered them.

'The best woman crime writer we have had since Sayers, Christie, Allingham and Marsh' *Edmund Crispin, Sunday Times*

'Ruth Rendell is at the very height of her powers. It will be an amazing achievement if she ever writes a better book' *Daily Express*

'This could become a classic among chillers' *H. R. F. Keating, The Times*

Bestselling Thriller/Suspense

☐ Hell is Always Today	Jack Higgins	£2.50
☐ Brought in Dead	Harry Patterson	£1.99
☐ Russian Spring	Dennis Jones	£2.50
☐ Fletch	Gregory Mcdonald	£1.95
☐ Black Ice	Colin Dunne	£2.50
☐ Blind Run	Brian Freemantle	£2.50
☐ The Proteus Operation	James P. Hogan	£3.50
☐ Miami One Way	Mike Winters	£2.50
☐ Skydancer	Geoffrey Archer	£2.50
☐ Hour of the Lily	John Kruse	£3.50
☐ The Tunnel	Stanley Johnson	£2.50
☐ The Albatross Run	Douglas Scott	£2.50
☐ Dragonfire	Andrew Kaplan	£2.99

Prices and other details are liable to change

ARROW BOOKS, BOOKSERVICE BY POST, PO BOX 29, DOUGLAS, ISLE OF MAN, BRITISH ISLES

NAME..

ADDRESS..

....

....

Please enclose a cheque or postal order made out to Arrow Books Ltd. for the amount due and allow the following for postage and packing.

U.K. CUSTOMERS: Please allow 22p per book to a maximum of £3.00.

B.F.P.O. & EIRE: Please allow 22p per book to a maximum of £3.00

OVERSEAS CUSTOMERS: Please allow 22p per book.

Whilst every effort is made to keep prices low it is sometimes necessary to increase cover prices at short notice. Arrow Books reserve the right to show new retail prices on covers which may differ from those previously advertised in the text or elsewhere.